DOC SAVAGE'S AMAZING CREW

William Harper Littlejohn, the bespectacled scientist who was the world's greatest living expert on geology and archaeology.

Colonel John Renwick, "Renny," his favorite sport was pounding his massive fists through heavy, paneled doors.

Lieutenant Colonel Andrew Blodgett Mayfair, "Monk," only a few inches over five feet tall, and yet over 260 pounds. His brutish exterior concealed the mind of a great scientist.

Major Thomas J. Roberts, "Long Tom," was the physical weakling of the crowd, but a genius at electricity.

Brigadier General Theodore Marley Brooks, slender and waspy, he was never without his ominous, black sword cane.

WITH THEIR LEADER, THEY WOULD GO ANYWHERE, FIGHT ANYONE, DARE EVERYTHING—SEEKING EXCITEMENT AND PERILOUS ADVENTURE!

Bantam Books by Kenneth Robeson
Ask your bookseller for the books you have missed

About Doc Savage:

DOC SAVAGE: HIS APOCALYPTIC LIFE
by Philip José Farmer

PIRATE OF THE PACIFIC

A DOC SAVAGE ADVENTURE

BY KENNETH ROBESON

BANTAM BOOKS
NEW YORK

PIRATE OF THE PACIFIC
*A Bantam Book / published by arrangement with
The Condé Nast Publications Inc.*

PRINTING HISTORY
Originally published in DOC SAVAGE MAGAZINE *July 1933*
Bantam edition / September 1967
2nd printing ..... August 1977

ISBN 0–553–11321–6

Published simultaneously in the United States and Canada

*Bantam Books are published by Bantam Books, Inc. Its trade-
mark, consisting of the words "Bantam Books" and the por-
trayal of a bantam, is registered in the United States Patent
Office and in other countries. Marca Registrada. Bantam
Books, Inc., 666 Fifth Avenue, New York, New York 10019.*

PIRATE OF THE PACIFIC

Chapter 1

THE YELLOW KILLERS

THREE laundry trucks stopped in the moonlight near a large commercial airport on Long Island. They made little noise. The machines bore the name of a New York City laundry firm.

The drivers peered furtively up and down the road. They seemed relieved that no one was in sight. Getting out, they walked slowly around the trucks, eyes probing everywhere, ears straining.

They were stocky, yellow-skinned, slant-eyed men. Their faces were broad and flat, their hair black and coarse. They looked like half-castes.

Satisfied, the three exchanged glances. They could see each other distinctly in the moonlight. No word was spoken. One driver lifted an arm—a silent signal.

Each Mongol dragged a dead man from the cab of his truck. All three victims had been stabbed expertly through the heart. They wore the white uniforms of laundry drivers, and on each uniform was embroidered the same name the trucks bore.

A roadside ditch received the three bodies.

Rear doors of the trucks were now opened. Fully a dozen Mongols and half-castes crawled out of the vehicles. They clustered beside the road.

Their faces were inscrutable; no muscle twitched, not a slant eye wavered. They were like a collection of placid, evil yellow images.

No weapons were in sight. But their clothing bulged suspiciously.

The first driver's arm elevated in another noiseless signal. The fellow seemed to be in charge.

The whole crowd glided quietly down the side road that led to the airport.

Plane hangars were an orderly row of fat, drab humps ahead. Faint strains of radio music came from one of them. A high fence of heavy woven wire encircled both hangars and plane runways.

1

Near the main gate in the fence, a guard lounged. His only movement was an occasional lusty swing at a night insect.

"These blasted mosquitoes are bigger'n hawks!" he grumbled, speaking aloud for his own company. "They must be flyin' over from the Jersey marshes."

The guard discerned a man approaching. He forgot his mosquitoes as he peered into the darkness to see who was approaching. When the man came within a few yards, the guard was able to distinguish his features.

"Hy'ah, yellow boy!" he grinned. "You can't poke around here at night. This is private property."

The Mongol replied with a gibberish that was unintelligible to the watchman.

"No savvy!" said the guard. "Splickee English!"

The Oriental came closer, gesturing earnestly with his hands.

The unfortunate guard never saw another figure glide up in the moonlight behind him. Moonlight flickered on a thick, heavy object. The weapon struck with a vicious, sidewise swipe.

The sound, as it hit, was like a loud, heavy *thump*. The guard piled down on the ground, out in a second.

THE other Mongols and half-castes now came up. They strode past the unconscious guard as though they hadn't seen him, passed through the gate in the high fence, and continued purposefully for the hangars.

No commands had been spoken. They were functioning like a deadly machine, following a deliberate plan.

Music from the radio was thumping a more rapid tempo—the musicians were working up to one of those grand slam endings. The radio instrument itself was a midget set, no larger than a shoe box.

Another night worker of the airport had plugged it into a power outlet on a workbench in a corner of the hangar. He lolled in the cockpit of a plane and listened to the music.

"Get hot!" he exhorted the radio, and beat time on the taut fuselage fabric with his palms.

Night traffic at this airport was negligible, and two men were the extent of the airport staff—this man, and the one at the gate.

The radio music came to an end. The station announcer introduced the next feature—a regular fifteen-minute news broadcast.

The man scowled and slouched more lazily in the plane

cockpit. He was not enthusiastic about this particular news broadcaster. The fellow handled the news in too dignified and conservative a fashion. He didn't set things afire.

"Good evening," said the radio commentator. "To-night, somewhere out on Long Island Sound, the under-the-polar-ice submarine, *Helldiver*, is coming. The craft was sighted by an airplane pilot shortly before darkness. She was headed toward New York.

"Arrival of the *Helldiver* in New York will bring to a close one of the most weird and mystifying adventures of modern days. The submarine left the United States many weeks ago, and vanished into the arctic regions. Approximately forty persons started the trip. Yet the craft is returning to-night with but six living men aboard, the others having perished in the polar wastes."

The man listened with more attention. This was quite a change from the news broadcaster's usual routine of foreign and political stuff.

Another fact made the news interesting and surprising to the listener. This was the first he had heard of the submarine *Helldiver*, on an expedition into the arctic regions. About forty had started out, and six were coming back!

Here was something worth listening to! Strange the papers had not carried a lot of ballyhoo about the start of the expedition! Explorers were usually anxious to get their pictures on the front pages.

The next words from the radio clarified this mystery.

"From the beginning, this polar submarine expedition has been a strangely secret affair," continued the commentator. "Not a newspaper carried a word of the sailing. Indeed, the world might still know nothing of the amazing feat, had several radio operators not tipped newspaper reporters that messages were being sent and received which disclosed the submarine was in the vicinity of the north pole. This information was something of a shock to the newspapermen. It meant they were losing out on one of the big news stories of the year. They had not even known the expedition was under way.

"During the last few days, there has been a great rush among newspapers striving to be first to carry a story of the expedition. They seem to be up against a blank wall. The men aboard the underseas boat sent word by radio that they wanted no publicity and that no story of the trip would be given out.

"Only two facts have been learned. The first is that but six men out of approximately forty are returning. The second bit of information was that the expedition is commanded by one of the most mysterious and remarkable men living in this day.

"That man is Doc Savage!"

THE news broadcaster paused to give emphasis to the name he had just pronounced.

The listening man was leaning over the cockpit edge, all interest. He did not see the yellow murder mask of a face framed in a small, open side door of the hangar. Nor did he see hands like bundles of yellowed bones as they silently lifted a strange death instrument and trained it on him.

"Doc Savage!" grunted the man. "Never heard of the guy!"

The voice from the radio continued. "Doc Savage is a man practically unknown to the public. Yet in scientific circles, he has a fame that is priceless. His name is something to conjure with.

"Last night, I was fortunate enough to attend a banquet given by scientific men here in New York. Many learned men attended. In the course of the evening, I heard references to important discoveries made by Doc Savage. The really bewildering thing about these discoveries was that they were made in widely different fields, ranging from surgery, chemistry, and electricity to the perfecting of a new, quick-growing species of lumber tree.

"Amazement seized me as I listened to eminent scientists discuss Doc Savage, the man of mystery, in the most glowing words. It seemed impossible they could speak in such terms of one man without exaggerating. Yet these were men certainly not given to exaggeration. I am going to give you a word picture of this man of mystery of whom they talked.

"Doc Savage is, despite his amazing accomplishments, a young man. He is a striking bronze giant of a figure. His physical strength, my informants assured me, is on a par with his mental ability. That means he is a marvel of muscular development. One of the scientists at the banquet told me in entire seriousness that, were Savage to enter athletic competition, his name would leap to the headlines of every paper in the country.

"This man of mystery has been trained from the cradle, until now he is almost a super being. This training, given by his father, was to fit Doc Savage for a definite purpose in life.

"That purpose is to travel from one end of the world to

the other, striving to help those who need help, punishing those who deserve punishment.

"Associated with Doc Savage are five men who love excitement and adventure, and who have dedicated themselves to their leader's creed of benefiting humanity.

"A strange and mysterious group of men, this! So unusual that the bare facts I am telling you now cannot but sound unreal and far-fetched. Yet I can assure you my information came from the most conservative and reliable sources."

The listening man blinked as he digested the words that came to his ears. "This Doc Savage must be quite a guy," he grunted.

Then the sneaking face was near. As unknowing as the watchman's companion at the gate, the man in the plane fell before the blow of the weapon, crumpled in his seat, unconscious or dead—the attacker did not look to see.

SLANT-EYED men poured into the hangar. No orders were uttered. The half-caste Orientals were still following their plan. Their efficiency was terrible, deadly. The whole group worked as one unit, an expert killing machine.

Two opened the hangar doors. Others busied themselves making four pursuit planes ready for the air. These ships were the most modern craft, yet the sinister men showed familiarity with the mechanism.

Three yellow raiders rushed up to the planes, carrying guns and bombs. The guns were quickly attached; the bombs were racked in clips on the undersides of the planes.

More men secured four parachutes from a locker room.

No time was wasted in scampering about the airport hunting for things. They knew exactly where everything was located.

The planes were strong-armed out of the hangars. Four Orientals dug goggles and helmets out of their clothing. The helmets were a brilliant red color.

The men cinched on the parachutes, then plugged into the cockpits. The scarlet helmets made them resemble a quartet of red-headed woodpeckers.

Exhaust thunder galloped across the tarmac as the motors started. Prop-streams tore dust from under the ships and pushed it away in squirming masses.

The planes flung along the runway, vaulted off, and slanted up into the now moon-whitened sky.

The Orientals who had been left behind lost no time in quitting the airport. Racing to the three laundry trucks, they entered, and drove hastily away.

Three or four minutes after the planes departed, no one

was left at the airport. The two watchmen lay where they had dropped, still unconscious. In the ditch beside the road sprawled the three slain drivers of the laundry trucks.

The adjacent countryside slept on peacefully. The four planes booming overhead attracted no attention, since night flying was not unusual even at this quiet port.

Within ten minutes, Long Island Sound was crawling under the craft. The surface of the Sound was like a faintly pitted silver plate, shimmering in the brilliant moonlight.

The planes spread out widely and flew low. Each Oriental pilot had high-magnification binoculars jammed to his eyes. With the same machine thoroughness which had stamped their bloody actions at the airport, they searched the Sound surface.

It was not long before they found what they sought—a narrow craft trailing across the Sound at the head of a long wedge of foaming wake.

The planes headed purposefully for this vessel.

Chapter 2

SEA PHANTOM

THE quarry came rapidly closer. More details of the craft were discernible. The half-caste Mongol pilots continued to use their binoculars. They tilted their planes down in steep dives toward the unusual vessel below.

It was a submarine. It resembled a lean-flanked, razorback whale several hundred feet long. Big steel runners extended from bow to stern, sled fashion. Amidships, a sort of collapsible conning tower reared.

The underseas craft floated high. On the bows, a lettered name was readable:

HELLDIVER.

It was this submarine which had been the subject of the radio news commentator's broadcast.

With deadly precision, the four planes roared down at the submersible. The Orientals had discarded their binoculars, and had their eyes pasted to the bomb sights. Yellow hands were poised, muscles drawn wire-hard, on bomb trips.

A naval bombing expert, knowing all the facts, would have

sworn the submarine didn't have a chance of escaping. It would be blown out of the water by the bombs.

The Mongol pilots were hot-eyed, snarling—yellow faces no longer inscrutable. They were about to accomplish the purpose of their bloody plot—the death of every one aboard the under-the-polar-ice submarine.

They got a shock.

From a dozen spots, the sub hull spewed smoke as black as drawing ink. Heaving, squirming, the dense smudge spread. It blotted the underseas boat from view, and blanketed the surface of the Sound for hundreds of feet in every direction.

With desperate haste, the Orientals deposited bombs in the center of the smoke mushroom. These explosions drove up treelike columns from the black body of the smoke mass. It was impossible to tell whether the sub had been damaged.

The four planes might have been angry, metallic bees droning over some gigantic, strange, black blossom, as they hovered watchfully. They did not waste more bombs, since the smoke cloud was now half a mile across. In it, the sub was like a needle in a haystack.

Several minutes passed. Suddenly, as one unit, the four planes dived for the western edge of the heavy smoke screen.

Their sharp eyes had detected a long, slender mass moving some feet beneath the surface. This was leaving a creamy wake.

In quick succession, the war planes struck downward at the object under the water. Four bombs dropped. The half-caste Mongols knew their business. Each bomb scored an almost perfect hit.

Water rushed high. The sea heaved and boiled. The concussions tossed the planes about like leaves.

Swinging in a wide circle, the planes came back. The commotion in the water had subsided. The pilots made hissing sounds of delight.

The long, slender mass was no longer to be seen. Oil filmed the surface. Oil such as would come from the ruptured entrails of a submarine.

THE pursuit planes whirled a half dozen lazy spirals. Convinced the deadly work was done, the leader of the quartet angled for the shore, four or five miles distant. Once over land, he dived out of the cockpit, fell a hundred feet, and opened his parachute. The plane boomed away. Eventually, it would crash somewhere.

Two other pilots followed their leader's example.

The third lingered a bit above the grisly smear of oil on the Sound surface.

He chanced to notice a small object near the cloud of black smoke. This seemed nothing more than a floating box. It bobbed lightly on the choppy waves.

The flyer ignored the box. It looked harmless—a piece of wreckage. A few moments later, he winged to shore and quitted his plane by parachute, as the others had done.

The man might have saved himself a lot of trouble had he taken time to investigate the floating box he had noted. Close scrutiny would have shown the top and sides of the box were fitted with what resembled large camera lenses.

Inside the box were other lenses, spinning disks perforated with small holes, sensitive photo-electric cells—a compact television transmitter. Waterproofed electric wires led from this down into the water.

Long Island Sound was not deep at this point. The under-the-polar-ice submarine, *Helldiver*, rested on the bottom. The wires from the television box entered the underseas boat.

Before the scanning disk of the television receiver in the sub, six men stood. They were a remarkable group. Six more unusual men than these probably had never assembled. Each possessed a world-wide reputation in his chosen profession.

There was "Renny," a hulking six feet four and two hundred and fifty pounds of him—with possibly fifty pounds of that weight concentrated in a pair of monster fists. Renny had a sober, puritanical face. About the only entertainment he permitted himself was knocking panels out of doors with his huge fists—a stunt he pulled at the most unexpected moments. As Colonel John Renwick, the engineer, Renny was known in many nations, and drew down fabulous fees when he worked.

There was "Long Tom," pale and none too healthy-looking, the weakling of the crowd in appearance. His looks were deceptive, though, as more than one big man had discovered. As Major Thomas J. Roberts, the electrical wizard, he had worked with the greatest electrical minds of his day.

"Johnny"—William Harper Littlejohn—was tall, gaunt, studious and bespectacled. He seemed half starved, with shoulders as bony as a coat hanger. Once he had headed the Natural Science department of a famous university. His knowledge of geology and archæology was profound. His books on these subjects were in every worthwhile library.

Two individuals stood on the edge of the group and scowled at each other like a cat and dog. They were "Monk" and "Ham." They always seemed on the point of flying at each other's throats. They swapped insults at every opportunity. Yet Ham had several times risked his life to save Monk, and Monk had done the same for Ham.

They were as unlike as men could be. Monk was a hairy monster of two hundred and sixty pounds, with arms some inches longer than his short legs, and a face incredibly homely. He was a human gorilla. The world of chemistry knew him as Lieutenant Colonel Andrew Blodgett Mayfair, one of the most learned chemists alive. But he looked dumb as an ox.

Ham was slender, lean-waisted. His clothing was sartorial perfection—tailors had been known to follow Ham down streets, just to see clothes being worn as they should be. His business cards read: "Brigadier General Theodore Marley Brooks," and he was possibly the most astute lawyer Harvard ever turned out. Ham carried a black cane of innocent aspect—a sword cane, in reality. He was never to be found without it.

The sixth member of the group was a mighty man of bronze—Doc Savage.

MAN of mystery, the radio commentator had labeled Doc Savage. Wizard of science! Muscular marvel!

The radio speaker had not exaggerated. Doc Savage was all of these things. His mental powers and strength were almost fantastic. He was the product of intensive expert, scientific training that had started the moment he was born.

Each day of his life, he had performed a two-hour routine of unusual exercise. Doc's powers might seem unbelievable, but there was really no magic about them. Rigid adherence to his exercise, coupled with profound study, was responsible.

Doc was a big man, almost two hundred pounds—but the bulk of his great form was forgotten in the smooth symmetry of a build incredibly powerful. The bronze of his hair was a little darker than that of his features, and the hair lay down tightly as a metal skullcap.

Most striking of all were the bronze man's eyes. They glittered like pools of flake gold when little lights from the television scanning disk played on them. They seemed to exert a hypnotic influence.

The lines of Doc's features, the unusually high forehead, the mobile and muscular and not-too-full mouth, the lean cheeks, denoted a power of character seldom seen.

"There goes the last of the flyers!" Doc said.

Doc's voice, although low, held a remarkable quality of latent power. It was an intensively trained voice—everything about Doc had been trained by his exercise routine.

"They sure enough thought it was the sub they had bombed," grinned Johnny, the bony archæologist. He adjusted the glasses he wore. These spectacles had an extremely thick left lens which was actually a powerful magnifying glass. Johnny, having practically lost the use of his left eye in the War, carried the magnifier there for handiness.

"Our contraption fooled them," Doc admitted. "But it might not have worked so well in daytime. A close look would have shown the thing was only a strip of canvas painted the color of steel, and some oil barrels, pulled along under the surface by a torpedo mechanism."

At the rear of the group, Monk stopped scowling at Ham long enough to ask: "You made that torpedo mechanism a couple of days ago—but how'd you know that early that something like this would happen?"

"I didn't know," Doc smiled faintly. "I only knew we were barging into trouble—and made preparations to meet it."

"If you was to ask me, we didn't have to barge into it," Monk grinned. "It came right out and grabbed us around the neck. Who were them guys who just tried to lay eggs on us?"

For answer, Doc Savage drew two radio messages from a pocket.

"You all saw the first one of these when it came," he said.

THE five men nodded. They had been far within the arctic regions when the first message had reached them by radio. It was very short, reading:

IN DESPERATE NEED OF YOUR HELP.
                              JUAN MINDORO.

Doc Savage had promptly turned the submarine southward. There was no need of lingering in the arctic, anyway. They had just completed the mission which had sent them into the polar regions—a desperate, adventurous quest for a fifty-million-dollar treasure aboard a derelict liner.

That treasure now reposed in the submarine—a hoard of

wealth that had threatened to cost its weight in the blood of men.

Doc had not told his five men what meaning Juan Mindoro's mysterious message might have. They had not asked questions, knowing he would tell them in good time. Doc was sometimes as much of a mystery to his five friends as he was to the rest of the world.

They had guessed there was danger ahead, however. Several days ago, Doc had hailed a liner they chanced to pass, and had put aboard the vessel three persons who were passengers on the submarine. These three people—a famous violinist and his wife and daughter—were, with Doc and his five men, the only survivors of the grisly episode in the arctic through which they had just passed.

The radio commentator had not mentioned these three. He had not known of them. Nor would he ever know, for the polar episode was now a closed book.

The fact that Doc had transferred the three passengers to the safety of a liner showed he wanted them out of danger—and told Doc's men they were headed for more trouble. They didn't mind. It was the thing they lived for. They went to the far corners of the earth to find it.

But they had not known Doc had received a second message from the same source.

Doc extended the missive. "I copied this myself a few days ago. Read it."

Crowding about, the five men read:

I HAVE BEEN FORCED TO GO INTO HIDING AT THE HOME OF THE MAN WHO WAS WITH ME WHEN I LAST SAW YOU. MEET ME THERE UPON YOUR ARRIVAL. AND BE PREPARED FOR ATTACKS ON YOUR LIFE.

JUAN MINDORO.

"Huh!" ejaculated Monk, wrinkling his flat, apish nose. "That don't tell us any more than the first one."

"Exactly," Doc replied. "And that explains why I have not informed you fellows what we're headed for. I don't know myself—except that it has something to do with the Orient.

"Juan Mindoro is a political power in the Pacific island group known as the Luzon Union. He is the most influential man in the island. And you know what recently happened to the Luzon Union."

"They were given their independence," said Ham. "I

remember now. Juan Mindoro had a big hand in electing the first president after the island group became self-governing. But what could that have to do with this?"

Doc shrugged. "It is too early to say."

He glanced at the television scanning disk. "The men who tried to bomb us are gone. We might as well get under way."

The submarine arose to the surface. The pall of black smoke still hung over the Sound.

Doc pulled in the television box which had been trailing the boat. Then the sub put on speed. It ran low in the water to escape attention from passing boats.

Once it dived to pass a launch loaded with newspaper reporters.

Chapter 3

THE MONGOL PERIL

PRACTICALLY every wharf in New York City was watched by newspaper reporters that night. The return of a submarine which had ventured under the polar ice was big news. The fact that those aboard the submarine wished no publicity made the story bigger. Each paper wanted to be the first to carry it.

Forty or so men had gone into the arctic—only six were coming back. A whale of a yarn! City editors swore over telephones at reporters. Photographers dashed about, answering false alarms turned in by news hawks who had mistaken rowboats and mud scows for the sub. Everybody lost a lot of sleep.

In a remote corner of the harbor, a rusty old tramp steamer swung at anchor. The captain of the ancient hulk, who was also the owner, happened to be an acquaintance of Doc Savage.

Shortly after midnight, this captain turned all of his crew out of their bunks. They fell to and made the submarine *Helldiver* fast alongside the tramp steamer. No one from land noted this incident.

A launch now sped ashore. It bore a small fortune in gold and diamonds—a load of the treasure Doc had brought back from the arctic. An armored car and a dozen guards with drawn guns met the launch and received the wealth. This also escaped the notice of the reporters.

The launch made more trips—until the whole treasure was on its way to an all-night bank.

Doc and his five men came ashore with the last load. Newspaper reporters would discover the submarine tied alongside the tramp steamer in the morning, but the tramp captain would profess mystification as to how it got there.

The whole arctic submarine expedition business was destined to be a mystery the news hawks would never solve.

A taxicab took Doc and his five men uptown. Doc rode outside, barehead, standing on the running board. He habitually did that when danger threatened. From this position, Doc's weird golden eyes missed very little—a sniper had hardly a chance of getting a shot at them before, he was discovered.

The cab halted before the most impressive building in the city. This skyscraper stabbed upward, a great white thorn of brick and steel, nearly a hundred stories.

Few people were on the sidewalk at this hour. But those who were, stopped and openly stared, such a striking figure did Doc Savage present. The big bronze man was a sensation wherever he went.

Doc and his five men rode an express elevator to the eighty-sixth floor of the skyscraper. Here Doc had his New York headquarters—a richly furnished office, one of the most complete libraries of technical and scientific tomes in existence, and an elaborately equipped chemical and electrical laboratory.

Doc had a second headquarters, fitted with another library and laboratory which were the most complete in existence. This, however, was at a spot he called his "Fortress of Solitude." No one knew its whereabouts. To this retreat Doc went at frequent intervals for the periods of intense study to which he devoted himself. At such times he vanished as completely as though he had dropped from the earth. No one could get in touch with him.

It was these periodic disappearances, as much as anything else, which had given Doc repute as a man of mystery.

MONK planted his furry bulk on a costly inlaid table in the office and began rolling himself a cigarette.

"Did you make arrangements by radio about the treasure?" he asked Doc. "I mean—about what the money is to be used for."

"That's all taken care of," the bronze man assured him.

They knew what that meant. The money was to be spent enlarging a weird institution which Doc maintained in up-state New York—a place where Doc sent all the criminals he captured. There, the lawbreakers underwent an amazing treatment in which their brains were operated upon and all memory of their past wiped out. Then they received training which turned them into useful citizens.

This unusual institution was Doc's own idea. He never sent a criminal to prison. They all went to the institution, to be operated upon by specialists whom Doc had trained. They were turned loose entirely reformed men—they didn't know they had ever been crooks.

"It's a little stuffy in here," complained Ham.

He crossed over and threw up the window. He stood there for a moment, staring at the impressive panorama of New York City spread out below. Then he turned away.

A moment later, a slate-colored pigeon fluttered up and landed on the window ledge. Doc and his men paid no particular heed. Pigeons were plentiful around the skyscrapers.

"What's our next move?" Ham wanted to know.

"You fellows scatter and attend to such of your private business as needs it," Doc suggested. "We've been gone several weeks, and no telling what we're headed for now. It may last longer."

"I got a secretary who takes care of my business," homely Monk grinned. "Better let me go with you, Doc."

Monk was proud of his secretary, maintaining she was the prettiest in New York.

"Nothing doing," said Doc. "There's no need of any army of us interviewing Juan Mindoro."

The slate-hued pigeon on the window ledge had not moved.

"You know where to find Juan Mindoro?" questioned Monk.

"His wireless message said he had gone into hiding at the home of the man who was with him when I saw him last," Doc replied. "I last met Juan Mindoro in Mantilla, the capital city of the Luzon Union. The man with him at the time was Scott S. Osborn, who is a sugar importer doing a large business in the Luzon Union trade. Osborn has a home near the north edge of the city. I'll go there."

Johnny had been squinting owlishly through his glasses which had the thick left lens—studying the pigeon. He took off his spectacles. As a matter of fact, he saw very well without them.

"That's what I call a sleepy pigeon!" he grunted. "It hasn't moved."

Doc glanced at the pigeon—his gaze became fixed.

Suddenly, a weird sound permeated the interior of the office; a trilling, mellow, subdued sound. It might have been the dulcet note of some exotic jungle bird, or the sylvan song of wind filtering through a leafless forest.

The strange trilling had the weird quality of seeming to come from everywhere within the office.

Electric tension seized Doc's five men. They knew what that sound meant. Danger!

For the sound was part of Doc—a small, unconscious thing that he did in moments of mental stress, or when he had made some astounding discovery, or when death threatened.

The pigeon abruptly flipped backward off the window sill.

Doc reached the window with flashing speed. The bird was some yards away, flying sluggishly. Doc watched until it was lost in the moonlight.

"That pigeon was where every word we spoke could reach it!" he said dryly.

"What if it was?" Monk snorted. "Pigeons can't tell what they hear."

"That one could."

"Huh?"

"It had a small microphone attached to its tail feathers."

MONK gaped after the departing pigeon. "For the love of Mike! But the thing flew away as though no wires were attached!"

"The wires were very small, about like silk threads," Doc declared. "They had to be small, or we would have seen them. A sharp jerk broke them, and left the bird free."

Leaning out of the window, Doc glanced up the sheer side of the skyscraper, then down. Only darkened windows met his gaze.

He examined the window ledge, noting bits of grayish powder. In a crack, he discovered a particle of cracked corn.

"The bird has been fed on the ledge!" he declared. "Either the office door was forced, or the grain was lowered from above. That was how it was taught to fly here."

He spun from the window, crossed the office. The speed with which his big bronze form moved was startling. He entered the corridor, glided down it to the end elevator. At his touch upon a secret button, the elevator door leafed back.

So quickly had Doc moved that his five men were still in the office. They piled out, big-fisted Renny in the lead, and joined Doc in the lift.

The cage sank them. It was a special installation, used only by Doc Savage, and geared at terrific speed. Such was the pace of descent that their feet were off the floor for the first sixty stories. Monk, Johnny, and Long Tom were wrenched to their knees by the shock of stopping.

"What I mean, that thing brings you down!" Monk grinned, getting up from all fours.

Monk had nearly worn out the high-speed elevator the first week after Doc had it installed, riding it up and down for the wallop he got out of it.

A cop was twiddling his nightstick out in front.

"See any one leave this neighborhood in a hurry within the last few minutes?" Doc demanded.

"No, sor," said the cop. "Sure, an' the only lads I've seen come out av a buildin' around here was two slant-eyed fellers. 'Twas in no hurry they were."

"Where'd they go?"

"Took a taxi."

Doc eyed his five friends.

"They must have been the men who sent us the pigeon," he told them. "They knew we'd discovered their trick, and fled. We'd be wasting time to hunt them."

Doc whirled back into the skyscraper.

His five men milled uncertainly, then trailed Doc. But the speed elevator was already gone. They rode a slower lift up to the eighty-sixth floor aerie, only to discover Doc had gotten whatever he had wanted from his laboratory, and had departed.

THE home of Scott S. Osborn, sugar importer, was a castlelike stone building perched atop a low hill in a wooded section of Pelham, one of the northern residential suburbs of New York City. The medieval castle architecture was carried out in a water-filled stone moat which surrounded the walls. A replica of a drawbridge, large enough for heavy automobiles to be driven across, spanned the moat.

Doc Savage arrived alone, driving a roadster which had the top entirely removed. The car was a reserved gray in color, but expensive, sixteen-cylindered. On a straight road, the machine could better a hundred and fifty an hour.

Doc alighted, crossed the drawbridge, and rang the bell.

No answer. An electric fixture cast pale light on the drawbridge.

He thumbed the bell again, received no response. The vast castle of a building was quiet as a tomb. The gatelike door was locked.

Doc returned to his roadster, got a black box somewhat larger than a good-sized suitcase, and carried it into the shrubbery near the drawbridge. On one end, the mysterious box had a cameralike lens. He pointed this at the drawbridge entrance, then silently plucked enough branches from near-by bushes to cover the box, hiding it thoroughly.

The moon shadows in the shrubbery swallowed his big bronze form. He made practically no sound, no stirring of leaves.

He reappeared again near one wall of the castle. The masonry was rough. He climbed to the top as easily as an ordinary man would walk a flat surface, although only the narrowest of ledges offered purchase to his tempered fingers.

For a moment, he poised at the top and reconnoitered. The same deathly silence gripped the mansion.

On either side were long, two-story buildings, their outer walls formed by the castle walls. In the center was a tiled court, a fountain, shrubbery, flowers. None of the windows were lighted.

Directly below Doc was a sheer drop of perhaps twenty-five feet. He sprang down—and so tremendously powerful were his leg muscles that the great leap hardly jarred him.

Moving swiftly, Doc tried a door. Locked. He sought another, then the rest, in quick succession.

Every door facing the court was secured.

Doc glided noiselessly into the shadows of the fountain. His fingers touched a box of an affair strapped under his coat. This was a bit greater in size than a cigar box. A switch on it clicked at his touch.

Doc plucked back his left coat sleeve. The object thus revealed looked at first glance like an enormous wrist watch. Closer scrutiny would have revealed a startling fact about the crystal of this watch.

It mirrored a very pale moving picture!

The scene was the drawbridge outside the castlelike dwelling of Scott S. Osborn, friend of Juan Mindoro. A shadowy figure stood on the drawbridge. His arms windmilled, gesturing orders to other vague forms.

The castle was being surrounded!

The oversize edition of a wrist watch on Doc's wrist, together with the box inside his coat, was a television receiver of marvelous compactness. It was tuned to the wavelength of a transmitter in the black box he had hidden under the brush outside the drawbridge.

Doc continued to watch the apparatus on his wrist. More slant-eyed men joined the one on the drawbridge. They carried revolvers, swords, knives. Two had deadly submachine guns.

One fitted a key in the lock of the gatelike door.

The faint click of the lock operating reached Doc's sensitive ears.

They must know he was inside. Probably they had seen him atop the wall. They were coming in, the murderous horde of them.

Chapter 4

THE DRIPPING SWORD

DOC SAVAGE quitted the murky vicinity of the fountain. He ran six light, springy paces. His bronze form shot upward in a tremendous leap. His corded fingers grasped the sill of a window which was open several inches. The window slid up. Doc slipped inside.

The whole thing had taken no more than a dozen ticks of the clock.

The drawbridge door opened. A group of half-caste Mongols skulked into the court, weapons bared for action.

The slant-eyed men poked about in the shrubbery until convinced Doc was not there. They tried the courtyard doors, and discovered them all locked.

"The bronze devil has gotten away!" one singsonged in his native tongue.

"That is impossible," replied the leader gravely. "Our lowly eyes beheld him upon the wall even as we arrived. He dropped inside." The man scowled at the high rear wall. "I marvel that the neck of the troublemaker was not broken."

"Then, oh mighty Liang-Sun Chi, he must have entered the house."

Liang-Sun Chi bent a bilious stare on the two sections of the residence.

"Is the bronze devil a magician, that he can go through locked doors and windows—for we left them all locked when we departed this afternoon."

"Only on the ground floor were they left locked, oh lord,"

answered the other. He pointed. "See! There is one second-floor window open."

The aperture the Mongol indicated was the identical window through which Doc Savage had entered. And Doc now stood in the darkened room behind, listening to the talk. He understood the language—it was one of scores he could handle as fluently as he spoke English.

"No kangaroo could leap that high, much less a man!" snorted Liang-Sun Chi. "But we will search this place well. It is said that the greatest mysteries have the simplest explanations. Perhaps we left a door open this afternoon."

He produced keys, unlocked one of the doors, and waved his men in. They entered cautiously, jabbing flashlight beams ahead.

Doc retreated from the window out of which he had been watching. He passed soundlessly through a door into a corridor. At the second step, his toe was stopped by a heavy object.

A flashlight came out of his pocket. It tossed a beam that was hardly more than a white thread.

The body of a man lay on the corridor floor. A sword slash had cleaved into his heart.

THE flash ray disclosed other details about the murder victim. He was an elderly man, at least sixty. He wore plum-colored knee breeches, white stockings, a braided coat with long tails, a powdered white wig—a very flashy butler's livery.

Doc examined more closely. The flunky had been dead several hours at least.

The Orientals were making considerable noise downstairs. Draperies ripped as they were torn down. Moving furniture grated on waxed floors.

"My sons, it is a wise man who gets all his troubles in front of him," called their leader, Liang-Sun Chi. "Search the basement."

Liang-Sun seemed to be something of a philosopher.

Working with silence and speed, Doc searched the upper floors. He found this side of the castle contained only servant quarters, gymnasium, indoor swimming pool, billiard rooms, and a few guest chambers.

Back at the open window, he glanced down. One of the guards left in the court stood directly below.

Doc returned to the second-floor corridor. At one end of this he had noted a suit of armor. The metal plates of the gear were supported on an iron framework. Inside the helmet was mounted a papier-mâché cast of a face. This did not differ greatly in color from Doc's tanned features.

There was no sound as Doc dislodged the armor from its pedestal. He carried it to the open window. It weighed fully a hundred pounds.

He tossed it down on the Mongol guard. The fellow was knocked cold and battered to the ground. The armor clanked loudly on the court tiles.

Men poured into the court. Yelling excitedly, they pounced on the armor. They thought Doc was inside.

None of them heard a window at the opposite end of the building lift, or saw a mighty bronze figure that flitted, silent as a great bat, across the court to the other house.

They speared swords into cracks in the armor. Chopping furiously, one half-caste got the helmet severed.

They saw they had been fooled.

"We are but dumb dogs!" Liang-Sun squawked. "We have brought shame to our ancestors! Continue the search!"

WHILE the Mongols pushed the murderous hunt a few yards away, Doc Savage scrutinized the other half of the vast mansion. He found no traces of Juan Mindoro, or Scott S. Osborn. In the library, however, he noted the floor cords had been wrenched from some of the reading lamps. Evidently these had served to bind prisoners.

Doc was now certain the Orientals had visited the castle some hours earlier. They had slain the butler. Probably they had made off with Juan Mindoro and Scott S. Osborn.

The Mongols finished with the other side of the house. They entered the room below Doc.

"It is said the lowly fly is never caught napping because he has eyes that see in all directions," Liang-Sun singsonged. "You will do well to imitate the fly, my sons. Should this bronze devil escape, some of us may lose our heads."

The flowery speech enlightened Doc on an important point. These Mongols and half-castes were serving some master—a master who wielded the power of life and death over them.

Their chief might be one of the pair who had listened in on the talk in Doc's office with the microphone-carrying pigeon, or the gist of the conversation might have been relayed to him. It was certain the talk the Mongols had overheard had brought them to Scott S. Osborn's home—for Doc had said he was coming here.

Two slant-eyed men mounted the stairs.

Doc located a light switch, clicked it. The fixtures remained dark. Doc recalled the wires torn from the reading lamps—fuses must have been blown when that was done.

The pair coming up the stairs exchanged whining whispers.

"Cold worms of fear are crawling up and down the spine of this insignificant person," one complained. "We have made many inquiries about Doc Savage, since we were so fortunate as to learn Juan Mindoro had appealed to him for help. We heard everywhere that Doc Savage was a mighty fighter. *Aie!* But no one told us he was a ghost. He must be lurking in this place, yet we have heard no sound and saw no one——"

"Swallow thy tongue, fool!" growled the other. "Only cowards talk of fear!"

"You are wrong. Only an idiot thinks not of danger——"

The Orientals had reached the top of the stairs. Now, without another word, one slowly lowered to his hands and knees. A moment later, he slouched prone on the hall carpet.

The second man eyed him foolishly. His lips writhed apart, showing teeth stained black from chewing betel nut. He seemed to be trying to cry out. Then he piled in a silent heap on the floor.

A giant, ghostly bronze figure, Doc Savage loomed over the pair. His fingers explored their clothing. He found nothing to indicate who their leader might be.

Both men snored as though asleep.

Doc retreated noiselessly down the second-floor corridor.

Liang-Sun droned words up from below. Receiving no answer from his two men, he mounted the stairs, flanked by three guardsmen and a machine gunner.

The outburst of cries as the two unconscious men were found sounded like the clamor that comes when a hawk flies into a flock of guineas.

A whispered consultation followed. Doc could not catch the words. The Orientals retreated to the lower floor, apparently to consider the situation.

"What manner of thing could have overcome our brothers?" Liang-Sun repeated over and over.

Suddenly, at the opposite end of the house, came a terrific uproar. Furniture overturned. Men gasped, cackled profanity.

"The bronze devil! He is here!" a man sang excitedly.

There was a loud clatter as the Mongols made for the noise.

Doc was puzzled. But it was too good a chance to pass up. He eased down a rear stairway, intent on quitting the place.

The stairs he chose let him into the lower floor library, a room walled with bookcases and floored with rich rugs.

The moment he stepped into it, he knew he had made a mistake. A dozen shadowy, slant-eyed men flung upon him.

THE noise at the other end of the house had been a trick to draw him down from upstairs.

The first leaping Mongol seemed to meet a bronze wall in mid-air. He was hurled back, and was impaled on the blunt sword of one who followed.

A second slant-eyed man got an open-handed slap that turned him over in the air like a Fourth-of-July pinwheel. Another found himself grasped about the chest. He shrieked, and the piercing shrillness of his voice was punctuated with the dull crack of breaking ribs.

The Mongols had not expected an easy fight. But they had not dreamed it would be like this. The giant bronze man moved with a speed that defied the eye. Sword slashes, delivered point-blank, sliced thin air. And when they did lay their hands on him, it was as if they had grasped living steel.

"He is not human!" wailed the man who had had his ribs broken.

More Orientals joined the fray. They blocked the doors. Flashlights came on. Time after time, light beams found the bronze giant, only to lose him.

A machine gun opened up, making a deafening gobble of sound in the room.

"Idiot!" Liang-Sun howled at the gunner. "Stop shooting! Do you want to kill us all?"

It was Liang-Sun who put a finish to the fray. He caught a momentary glimpse of Doc. The bronze man stood in the center of a large rug. Dropping swiftly, Liang-Sun seized the rug and yanked. Doc was brought down.

Liang-Sun flung the rug over Doc in a big fold.

"Are you snails that you cannot help me!" he squawled at his men.

A brisk twenty seconds followed—and they got Doc rolled up like a mummy in the rug. They brought tire chains from the garage and tied them securely about the rug.

Liang-Sun was proud of himself. He beat his chest with a fist.

"Single-handed, I did more than the rest of you dogs!" he boasted.

He plucked open one end of the rug roll and threw his flash beam inside.

He could see Doc's face. The bronze features bore absolutely no expression. But the cold fierceness in the strange golden eyes made Liang-Sun drop the rug folds and stand up hastily.

"Half of you go outside, my sons," he commanded. "Should any one be drawn here by sounds of the fighting, kill them. This house stands alone, and probably the sounds were not heard. But if any one comes, show them that curiosity is indeed a fatal disease."

A part of the Orientals hurried out into the moon-bathed court.

"Watch the prisoner closely!" Liang-Sun directed the others. "If he should escape, I can promise there will be heads lopped off. I am going to call the master to see what he wants to do with the bronze devil."

LIANG-SUN strode through rooms, playing his flash beam about, until he located a telephone. He swept the instrument up with a flourish.

When the phone operator's voice came, Liang-Sun spoke in English. He handled the language well enough, except that, Chinese fashion, he turned all the "R's" into "L's."

"Give me numbel Ocean 0117," he requested.

It was almost a minute before he got his party. He recognized the singsong voice at the other end of the wire. Without delay, he launched rapid words in his native tongue.

"We have secured the merchandise after which we came, oh lord," he said. "We now have it rolled in a rug and bound securely. This lowly person wishes to know how you want it delivered."

"In two pieces, dumb one!" rasped the voice in the receiver. "Cut the merchandise in two in the middle. Then you may leave it there. I have other work for you to do."

"My understanding of your wishes is perfect. What is this other work?"

"The sugar importer, Scott S. Osborn, has a brother who lives up on Park Avenue. We are holding merchandise which this brother might be greatly interested in buying."

"I understand, oh lord. No doubt, Scott S. Osborn's brother will indeed want to purchase our merchandise."

The two were speaking in vague terms, lest a phone

operator be listening. But they understood each other perfectly. They had Scott S. Osborn prisoner, and were going to try to ransom him to his brother.

"This sale of merchandise is not extremely important," continued the voice over the wire. "But since we are holding the goods, we might as well take a profit. You will visit the brother and seek the best price you can obtain."

"I comprehend most clearly, oh lord. Exactly where does Scott S. Osborn's brother live, that I may find him without trouble."

"Get the address from the phone book, dumb one!"

"I shall do that."

"Returning to the subject of the merchandise you have wrapped in the rug—you are perhaps aware there are five others of a similar pattern, although of lesser importance. We may find it desirable to seek them also. But I shall discuss that with you at a later time. Cut the goods you have in two pieces. Do so at once."

Liang-Sun singsonged that he understood. He hung up the receiver, drew his sword, and swung into the room where Doc Savage had been captured.

The rolled rug had not moved. The slant-eyed guards sat about the room, lost in the shadows. But their flash beams blazed upon the rug.

Liang-Sun sprang forward, sword uplifted.

"Behold, dogs!" he shouted. "I will show you how a master swings his blade."

The sword hissed down.

Rolled rug—the body within it—were chopped neatly in halves.

A ghastly crimson flood spurted from the rug and washed over the floor.

LIANG-SUN callously wiped his blade. "Never, my sons, will you see a man cut in halves in more expert fashion!" he addressed his men.

He got no answer.

The half-caste leader stared about. He seemed to lose inches in height. His eyes bloated out from behind their sloping lids.

"Have your tongues been eaten, that you do not answer?" he gulped.

Leaping to the nearest Mongol, Liang-Sun shook him. The man toppled out of his chair. Liang-Sun jumped to another, a third, a fourth.

All were unconscious!

With mad haste, Liang-Sun shucked the rug off the head and shoulders of the man he had cut in two.

Liang-Sun's squawl of horrified surprise was like that of a cat with its tail stepped on.

The body in the rug was one of his own men!

Terror laid hold of Liang-Sun, a fright such as he had never before experienced. He dashed headlong out into the court.

"The bronze man is a devil!" he shrilled. "Flee, my sons!"

The Orientals who had been on guard outside, needed no urging. They battled each other to be first across the draw-bridge and into their cars. They had their fill of fighting the bronze giant.

They departed without knowing what had made their fellows unconscious. A close inspection of the room where the men slept would have shown the remains of many thin-walled glass balls. Perhaps they might have guessed these had originally contained an anæsthetic gas which made men unconscious the instant they breathed it, yet which became harmless after it had been in the air two or three minutes.

These anæsthetic globes were Doc's invention. He always carried a supply with him.

Cars bearing the fleeing Mongols were not out of earshot when Doc arose from the concealment of a divan not six feet from the phone over which Liang-Sun had talked to his chief.

Doc had heard that conversation.

Doc's escape from the tightly chained rug, so mystifying to Liang-Sun, had not been difficult. Doc had employed a simple trick used by escape artists. He had tensed all his muscles when the rug was being tied. Relaxing later, he had plenty of room to crawl out after he had reduced the guards to unconsciousness with the anæsthetic.

Doc had not been affected by the anæsthetic for the simple reason that he could hold his breath during the two or three minutes it was effective.

He sped out of the castle, with the idea of following Liang-Sun and the others. But they had stolen his gray roadster.

Doc ran for the nearest boulevard. It was a quarter of a mile distant. Had official timers held stop watches on that quarter, the time Doc did it in would have been good for a headline on any sport page in the country. But the only observer was a stray dog which sought to overhaul the bronze man.

On the boulevard, Doc hailed a taxi.

Chapter 5

THE DRAGON TRAIL

THE cab let Doc Savage out before an uptown New York police station. He entered. The marked deference of the cops, the celerity with which they sprang to grant his wishes, showed they knew him as a person of power. The police commissioner himself would not have gotten better service.

A "back number" telephone directory was produced. This listed the phone numbers, and the names to which they belonged, rather than the name followed by a number, as in an ordinary directory.

Doc looked up the number Liang-Sun had called—Ocean 0117. It was listed as the:

DRAGON ORIENTAL GOODS CO.

The address was on Broadway, far south of the theatrical portion of the street known as the Great White Way.

Doc took a cab downtown. The hack driver wondered all the way why his passenger rode the running board of the taxi, rather than inside. The hackman had never before had a thing like that happen.

The building, housing the Dragon Oriental Goods Company, was a shabby, ten-story structure. It was decorated in the ornate fashion popular thirty years ago. "The Far East Building," a sign said.

Chinatown lay only a few blocks away.

Directly across the street, a new forty-story skyscraper was going up. The steel framework of this was nearing completion. A night force of men was pushing construction. Noise of riveting machines banged hollowly against near-by structures and throbbed in the street.

A dusty directory told Doc the Dragon concern occupied a tenth-floor office.

An elevator, driven by a man in greasy tan coveralls, was in operation. The fellow's round moon of a face and eyes sloping slightly upward at the outer ends advertised that some of his recent ancestors had come from the Far East.

This man never saw Doc enter. The bronze giant walked up. He did not want to advertise his presence—the elevator operator might get word to whoever was leading the Mongol horde.

The office of the Dragon Oriental Goods Company faced the front of the building. The door lock yielded readily to a thin steel hook of an implement from Doc's pocket. He entered.

No one was there.

For furniture, the place had a couple of desks, worn chairs, filing cabinets. Desk drawers and filing cabinets were empty. There was not a sheet of paper in the place. No finger prints were on the telephone, desk, window shade, or doorknob.

The window was dirty. Across the street, the girders of the building under construction made a pile like naked brush. The *drum-drum* of riveters was a somber song.

The elevator operator did not see Doc quit the building.

HALF an hour later, Doc entered his eighty-sixth-floor skyscraper office uptown.

He was surprised to find none of his five friends there. He consulted one of the elevator boys.

"They all five went out a few minutes ago to get something to eat," explained the youth.

"When they come back, tell them I was here," Doc directed.

He did not depart immediately, though. His next actions were unusual.

From a pocket, he took a bit of colorless substance shaped like a crayon. He wrote rapidly on his office window with this—putting down a lengthy message.

Yet when he finished, there was no trace of what he had written. Even a magnifying glass would not have disclosed the presence of the writing.

The elevator carried him down to the street. He walked away rapidly.

Some ten minutes later, his five men returned. Their faces mirrored the satisfaction of men who had just eaten a hearty shore dinner after some weeks of dining in the grease-soaked interior of a submarine.

"I missed the pint of grease I've had to take with my meals recently," Monk grunted contentedly. Then he leered at Ham. "Them pigs' knuckles and sauerkraut was swell!"

The distinguished, snappily clad Ham scowled at hairy Monk. Any mention of pigs that Monk made was sure to aggravate Ham. This hearkened back to a couple of incidents in the War.

Ham had taught Monk certain highly insulting French words, and told him they were just the thing to flatter a French general with. Monk had used them—and landed in the guardhouse.

Monk had barely been released when there occurred one of the most embarrassing incidents of Ham's career. He was hailed up on a charge of stealing hams. Somebody had framed him!

To this day, Ham hadn't been able to prove the framing was Monk's work. That rankled. Especially since Ham had received his nickname from the incident; a nickname he didn't care for in the least.

"After the way you stuffed yourself, I have hopes!" Ham snapped.

"Hopes of what?" Monk queried.

"That you'll croak of indigestion!"

The elevator operator spoke up eagerly when he saw them.

"Mr. Savage was here, and has gone," he said.

Doc's five men exchanged sharp glances. They lost no time getting up to the eighty-sixth floor.

LONG TOM, the scrawny-looking electrical wizard, hurried into the laboratory. He came out with an apparatus which might easily be mistaken for an old-time magic lantern.

The lights were switched off. Long Tom flicked a switch on his machine. He pointed at the window on which Doc had written.

Doc's message sprang out on the darkened windowpane. Glowing with a dazzling electric blue, its appearance was uncanny.

Long Tom's apparatus was simply a lamp which projected strong ultra-violet light rays. The substance with which Doc had written on the window, although invisible to the naked eye, would glow in eerie fashion in the ultra-violet light.

It was by this method that Doc habitually left messages for his men.

The five read the communication. Doc's handwriting, machinelike in its perfection, was as easy to read as newsprint:

Here is your job, Ham: The Mongols are holding Juan Mindoro and his friend, Scott S. Osborne. A messenger will visit Osborn's brother, to demand a ransom.

Your work as a lawyer has probably brought you in contact with the family attorney of Osborn's brother, so you should be able to work through him and persuade them to pay the ransom demanded. We will then follow the man to whom it is paid.

But do not follow the messenger who demands it.

"This will be a cinch," Ham declared, spinning his sword cane adroitly. "I happen to be quite well acquainted with that attorney. Incidentally, he is the lawyer of both Scott S. Osborn and his brother."

"Shut up!" Monk grunted insultingly. "Don't you think we want to read the rest?"

They deciphered the remainder of the instructions in silence:

Monk, Renny, Long Tom, and Johnny will go to Scott S. Osborn's home north of town. The place is built like a medieval castle. Inside are perhaps a dozen Mongols and half-castes. You will ship them to our institution, then come back here and wait.

"Holy cow!" Renny was bewailing. "There won't be any excitement in our part of it!"

Monk's big grin was crowding his ears.

"I got hopes, though!" he chuckled. "If Doc has bagged that many men this early in the game, it shows we've tackled something that is plenty big. We may get our feet wet yet!"

Monk was no prophet. His feet wet! He'd be deep enough in trouble to drown, before long. But he had no way of knowing that.

HAM watched the others depart to ship the Orientals Doc had captured to the up-state institution, where they would receive the effective, if unusual, treatment that would turn them into honest men.

A telephone call put Ham in touch with the elderly lawyer who served Scott S. Osborn and his brother. Ham explained what he desired.

"The family might hesitate about complying with the wishes of a stranger," he finished. "It would help greatly if you would sort of put the O.K. on me. I am, of course, working for the interest of your clients."

"I'll do better than that!" declared the other attorney. "I shall be at the home of Osborn's brother when you arrive. When I advise them of the situation, I am sure they will do as you desire."

"That will be great," Ham assured him.

Ham hurried to his bachelor quarters, in a club which was one of the most luxurious in the city, although not widely known. The members were all wealthy men who wished to live quietly.

A change of clothing was the object of Ham's visit. He donned formal evening garb, secured a more natty-looking sword cane from a collection he kept on hand, and took a taxi to the home of Scott S. Osborn's brother.

The dwelling was large. It might have been mistaken for a small apartment building.

Dismissing his taxi, Ham mounted the steps. He was about to ring the bell when his hand froze.

A stream of scarlet was crawling slowly from under the door.

Ham listened. He could hear nothing. He tried the knob. It turned, but the door, after opening about two inches, would go no farther. Ham shoved. He could tell that he was pushing against a body lying on the floor inside.

He got the panel half open, put his head in cautiously.

The vestibule was brilliantly lighted. No living person was in sight.

The body of the old lawyer whom Ham had called not many minutes ago, had been blocking the door. The elderly man had been stabbed at least fifteen times.

Ham, his sword cane ready, stepped inside. The weight of the dead man against the door shoved it shut. The lock clicked loudly.

As though that were a signal, a man hurtled from a near-by door.

The fellow was chunky, lemon-complected, sloping of eye. His face was a killer mask. He waved a sword.

It was Liang-Sun, although Ham didn't know that, not having seen him before.

Liang-Sun got a shock when Ham unsheathed the slender, rippling steel blade of his sword cane. Ham's blade leaped out hungrily.

With desperate haste, Liang-Sun parried. He was surprised, but still confident. Among the fighting men of Mongolia and China, he had been considered quite a swordsman.

Ten seconds later, Liang-Sun's confidence leaked out like water from a gunnysack. The air before his face had apparently turned into a whistling hell of sharp steel. A chunk of his hat brim was sliced off and fluttered away.

Liang-Sun felt like a man clubbing a swarm of hornets with a stick. Backing up, he sought to haul a revolver from his coat pocket with his left hand. He hadn't wanted to use the gun before, because of the noise. But he would be glad to do so now.

A dazzling slash of Ham's sword cut the whole skirt and pocket from Liang-Sun's coat, and the revolver bounced away.

STEEL whined, clashed, rasped. Both fighters sought to get to the revolver. Neither could quite do it.

Liang-Sun felt a tickling sensation across his stomach. He looked down and saw his clothing had been slit wide. Another inch would have finished him.

He backed away swiftly, passing through the door from which he had leaped. Ham followed, cutting and parrying briskly.

A man was sprawled across a table in the room. He had white hair, ruddy features. He, too, had been stabbed to death.

Ham had seen the man once before, perhaps a year ago. It was the brother of Scott S. Osborn.

A wall safe gaped open.

On the table with the dead man lay a heap of jewels, rings, currency.

This explained the situation to Ham.

The Mongol messenger had come to demand ransom, had seen the money, and decided a bird in hand was better than one in the bush. He had slain and robbed Osborn's brother, rather than bother with ransom.

The poor old lawyer out by the door had been murdered when he arrived.

White with rage, Ham redoubled his sword play.

Liang-Sun fairly ran backward. A sudden spring put him through a door. He slammed it. Ham pitched against the panel. It resisted.

Seizing a chair, Ham battered the door down. He ran across a dining room, then a kitchen. A rear door gaped open beyond. It let him into an alleylike court. There was only one exit from this, a yawning space between two buildings, to the right.

An indistinct, rapidly moving figure dived into this opening.

Ham pursued. He pitched headlong between the buildings, came out on the walk, and saw his quarry scuttle under a street lamp at the corner.

Ham set out after him—only to bring up sharp as a powerful voice came to him from a near-by door recess.

"I'll follow him, Ham!" the voice said.

It was Doc Savage.

Ham understood, then, why Doc had directed, in the message on the skyscraper window, that the ransom-demanding courier was not to be followed. Doc intended to do the trailing, hoping to be led to the master mind who was behind all this callous, inhuman bloodletting.

In order not to make the fleeing Oriental suspicious, Ham continued his chase. But at the first corner, he deliberately took the wrong turn.

When he came back, there was no sign of Doc or the half-caste Mongol.

Chapter 6

THE STOLEN GLASS

At the precise moment Ham was wondering about them, Doc and Liang-Sun were five blocks distant. Liang-Sun was just climbing the steps of a Third Avenue elevated station.

The Mongol had lived much of his life in violence, and knew enough to watch his back trail. He saw nothing suspicious. He kept wary eyes on the stairway until a train came in. Even after he boarded the almost deserted train, he watched the platform he had just quitted, as well as the one on the other side of the tracks. He saw no one—not a single other passenger got aboard.

He should have watched the rear platform. Doc was already ensconced there. He had climbed a pillar of the elevated a short distance above the station and run down the tracks.

The train clanked away southward, disgorging a few passengers at each stop.

At Chatham Square, very close to Chinatown, Liang-Sun alighted. To make sure no one got off the train after him who seemed in the least suspicious, he waited on the platform until the cars pulled out. Greatly relieved, he finally descended.

Doc Savage, having slid down a pillar of the elevated, was waiting for him, seated in some one's parked car.

Liang-Sun walked rapidly toward the Oriental section. He passed two sidewalk peddlers who, even at this late hour, were offering for sale filthy trays of melon seeds and other celestial dainties.

A moment later, Doc Savage also sauntered past the peddlers.

Both venders of melon seeds and dainties shoved their trays of merchandise in the handiest waste can and followed Doc. Their hands, folded across their stomachs, fingered large knives in their sleeves. Their faces, the color of old straw, were determined.

Doc did not look back. Several times, he glanced down at his hands swinging at his sides. In the palm of each hand was a small mirror.

The mirror showed him the two who haunted his trail.

Doc's bronze features held no feeling as he watched. This master of the Mongols was clever in having men follow Liang-Sun to see that no one dogged his tracks.

Gone were any hopes Doc had of locating the master mind through Liang-Sun—unless he could be induced to talk by force.

Doc's left hand wandered casually into his pocket, drew out four of the glass balls filled with anæsthetic. Holding his breath, Doc dropped them. They shattered, releasing the colorless, odorless vapor.

Doc strode on.

Behind him, the two peddlers walked into the anæsthetic. They fell forward on their faces, nearly together.

LIANG-SUN chanced to turn around at this moment. He saw Doc, saw what had happened. His piping yell of fright sounded like a rat squeal in the dingy Chinatown street. He fled.

A bronze blur of speed, Doc raced after him.

Liang-Sun was fumbling inside the waistband of his trousers. He brought out his sword. Evidently he carried it in a sheath strapped next to his leg.

Doc overhauled him rapidly. The Mongol was only a hundred feet away—seventy-five—fifty.

Then a big policeman, attracted by Liang-Sun's yell of fear, popped around a corner. He stood directly in Liang-Sun's path, revolver in hand.

The Mongol was desperate. He slashed his sword at the cop—and the cop shot him, killing him instantly.

The policeman had acted instinctively in defense of his life. He watched Doc come up.

"Sure, an' this is the first man I ever killed. I hope he needed it," the cop spoke.

He eyed Doc suspiciously. He did not know the bronze giant.

"Was ye chasin' this bird?" he demanded.

"I was," Doc admitted. "And don't let the fact that you killed him bother you. He is a murderer, probably several times over. He killed a man at the home of Scott S. Osborn to-night. And I think he must have committed other crimes at the residence of Scott S. Osborn's brother not very many minutes ago."

Doc did not know what had happened in the dwelling of Scott S. Osborn's brother. But the fact that Ham had chased Liang-Sun out showed something had gone wrong.

The cop was suspicious of Doc.

"Yez jest stick around here, me b'y!" he directed. "We'll want to ask yez a lot av questions."

Doc shrugged.

The officer slapped big hands over Doc's person in search of a gun. The fact that he did that was unfortunate. He broke one of the anæsthetic balls in Doc's pockets.

A minute afterward, he was stretched on his back on the walk, snoring loudly.

Doc left the cop where he lay. The fellow would revive after a time, none the worse for his slumber.

From a near-by call box, Doc turned in an alarm to the police station. He did not give his name.

He hurried back to get the two peddlers who had been following him. They should be asleep on the walk.

But they weren't! Some denizen of Chinatown had moved them. Doc knew it must have been the work of some of the Mongol horde.

Chinatown, despite all the fiction written about it, was actually one of the quietest sections in the city. No legitimate resident of the district would court trouble by assisting the unconscious pair.

A brief, but intensive search disclosed no sign of the vanished two.

HALF an hour later, Doc was in his skyscraper office uptown. None of his five men had returned.

With a chemical concoction from the laboratory, Doc erased the invisible writing off the window. Then he inscribed a fresh message there.

Swinging out into the corridor, he rode the button until an elevator came up. The cage doors opened noiselessly, let him in, and closed. There was a windy sigh of a sound as the lift sank.

Adjoining Doc's office was a suite which had been empty

some months. Rents were high up here in the clouds, and times were tough, so many of the more costly offices were without tenants.

It would have taken a close examination to show the door of this adjoining suite had been forced open.

Inside, a man was just straightening from a large hole which had been painstakingly cut in the wall of Doc's office. The actual aperture into Doc's sanctum was no larger than a pin head. But by pressing an eye close, an excellent view could be obtained.

The watcher was a round-faced, lemon-skinned Oriental. He hurried out and tried to force the door of Doc's office. The lock defied him. The door was of heavy steel—Doc had put that steel in to discourage Renny's joyful habit of knocking the panels out with his huge fists.

Returning to the vacant suite, the Oriental set to work enlarging his peep-hole. He used an ordinary pick. In ten minutes, he had opened an aperture in the plaster and building tile which would admit his squat frame.

He crawled in. First, he made sure the corridor door could be locked from the inside. He left it slightly ajar.

The window next received his attention. He had watched Doc write upon it. Yet he could discern no trace of an inscription.

Working with great care, the Mongol removed the pane of glass. He carried it outside. He was going to take it to a place where some one with an understanding of invisible inks could examine it. He rang for the elevator.

The elevator operator eyed him doubtfully as they rode down.

"You work here?" he demanded.

"Wolk this place allee time now," singsonged the Mongol. He grinned, wiped his forehead. "Allee same wolk velly much and get velly little money."

The operator was satisfied. He hadn't seen this man before. But who would go to the trouble of stealing a sheet of plate glass?

The cage stopped at the ground floor. The Mongol bent over to pick up his glass.

What felt like a steel trap suddenly got his neck.

THE slant-eyed man struggled desperately. The hands on his throat looked bigger than gallon buckets.

They were Renny's hands—paws that could knock the panel out of the heaviest wooden door.

Monk, Long Tom and Johnny danced about excitedly outside the elevator. They all had just come in.

"Hey!" Monk barked. "How d'you know he's one of the gang?"

They were nearly as surprised as the Mongol at Renny's sudden act.

"He's got the window out of Doc's office, you homely goat!" Ham snapped, after a glance into the elevator.

"Yeah!" Monk bristled. "How can you tell one hunk of glass from another?"

"That is bullet-proof glass," Ham retorted. "So far as I know, Doc has the only office in this building with bullet-proof windows."

Monk subsided. Ham was right.

Renny and the Oriental were still fighting. The Oriental launched frenzied blows, but he might as well have battered a bull elephant, for all the effect they had.

Desperate, the Mongol clawed a knife out of a hidden sheath.

"Look out, Renny!" Monk roared.

But Renny had seen the knife menace. He hurled the slant-eyed man away. The fellow spun across the tiled floor. He kept a grip on his blade.

Bounding to his feet, he drew back his arm to throw the knife.

Wham! A gun had appeared magically in Long Tom's pale hand, and loosed a clap of a report.

The bullet caught the Mongol between the eyes and knocked him over backward. His knife flew upward, point-first, and embedded in the ceiling.

A cop, drawn by the shot, ran in, tweeting excitedly on his whistle.

There was no trouble over the killing, though. Long Tom, as well as Monk, Renny, Ham and Johnny, held high honorary commissions in the New York police force.

Within a quarter of an hour, the five were up in the eighty-sixth floor office examining the pane of glass with ultra-violet light.

The message Doc had written upon it, flickered in weird bluish curves and lines. They read:

To RENNY: The chief of this Mongol gang sometimes uses an office listed under the name of the Dragon Oriental Goods Co. It is the center, front office on the tenth floor of the Far East building on lower Broadway. A new skyscraper is going up across the street.

Your engineering training will enable you to get a structural-steelworker's job on the new building, Renny. Watch the office of the Dragon Oriental Goods Co., and trail any one you see using it.

With the chemical eraser, Monk carefully cleaned the glass plate. They were taking no chances on the leader of the Mongols getting hold of it. Such a misfortune might mean Renny's finish.

"We'll drop around sometime and watch you doing a little useful labor on that building," Monk grinned at Renny.

Chapter 7

DEATH TRAIL

RENNY had been working as a structural steel man for half a day. He was operating a riveting gun on what would eventually be the tenth floor of the new building. In his monster hands the pneumatic gun was a toy.

None of the other workers knew why he was here, not even the job foreman. Renny had come with such excellent references that he had been given a job instantly. The quality of his work had already attracted favorable attention. The crew foreman was proud of his new recruit.

"Stick with us, buddy, and you'll get ahead," the foreman had told Renny confidentially. "We can use men like you. I'll see that you get a better job at the end of the week."

"That'll be fine!" Renny replied.

Not a muscle of Renny's sober, puritanical face changed during this conversation. The crew foreman would probably have fallen off the girder on which he was standing, had he known Renny had handled engineering jobs for which he had been paid a sum sufficient to buy a building such as this would be when finished.

At lunch hour, most of the workers went to near-by restaurants to eat. But Renny consumed a sandwich, remaining near where he had been working.

Renny didn't want to lose sight, even for a short time, of the office of the Dragon Oriental Goods Company. And it was during the lunch hour that his watch produced results.

A lemon-skinned fellow entered the tenth-floor office. His actions were unusual. Producing a rag from his clothing, the

Oriental went over every object in the room which might have been handled, polishing it briskly.

"Making doubly sure no finger prints were left behind!" Renny told himself. "I'll just trail that bird."

Throwing away the wrapper of the sandwich he had consumed, Renny stretched lazily and remarked to another steel worker smoking near by: "Think I'll go get some hot coffee."

He descended.

Within ten minutes, the man who had been in the Dragon Oriental Goods Company office put in his appearance. A close look showed Renny he was one of the half-castes, an admixture of Mongol and some other race.

The fellow boarded one of the open street cars which ran down Broadway. This vehicle had no sides, only a roof. Passengers simply stepped aboard wherever was handiest.

Renny followed in a taxi. He slouched low in his seat, hoping his work-stained clothing and greasy cap would help him escape detection. Renny had wiped off the motor of his automobile with the garments, before going to his new job. This gave them the proper coating of grime.

The quarry alighted near Chinatown. He soon passed a shabby Celestial walking up and down the street with a sign on his chest and another on his back, advertising a chop-suey restaurant.

No sign of recognition did Renny's quarry and the sandwich man exchange, yet the sandwich man studied Renny most intently—and was very careful Renny did not notice.

The fellow then scuttled down a side street.

Renny continued his shadowing, unaware of this incident.

THE half-caste Mongol turned into a little shop which seemed to sell everything from edible bamboo shoots to cloisonné vases. He puchased a small package of something, then came out. He began to chew some of the package contents.

He might have given a message to the shop proprietor, or received one. Renny could not tell.

The Mongol breed's next move was to enter—of all things—a radio store.

Renny sauntered past the front. No one was visible within the store; not even the proprietor. Renny hesitated, decided to take a chance, and entered.

There was a door in the back. Listening, Renny heard nothing. He opened and shut his enormous hands uneasily.

Finally, he shucked an unusual pistol from under one arm-
pit.

This gun was only slightly larger than an ordinary automatic, but it was one of the most efficient killing machines ever
invented. Doc had perfected the deadly weapon—an extremely compact machine gun. It fired sixty shots so rapidly
it sounded like the bawl of a great bull fiddle, and it could be
reloaded in the time required to snap a finger.

Renny shoved the rear door open. A gloomy passage
yawned beyond. He stepped in.

The door wrenched out of his hand and shut with a bang,
actuated by strong levers. The inner side of the door was
plated with sheet steel.

Renny darted his machine gun at the panel, locked the
trigger back, and flipped the muzzle in a quick circle. The
gun made a deafening moan; empty cartridge cases rained to
the floor by scores.

Renny snarled hoarsely. The bullets were barely burying
themselves in the steel. It was armor plate.

Whirling, he plunged down the passage. Black murk lay
before him. He shoved out the machine gun, threw a brief
spray of lead. He was taking no chances.

Into another door, he crashed. It, too, had a skin of armor
plate.

Renny carried a small waterproof cigarette lighter, although he did not smoke. It was handier than matches. He
brushed this aflame with his thumb and held it high.

Walls and floor were solid timbers. The ceiling was pierced
with slits. They were about two inches wide, and ran the
entire passage length.

An iron rod, more than an inch in diameter, delivered a
terrific slashing blow through one of these cracks. Dodging,
Renny barely got clear.

Crouched to one side, he heard the rod strike again and
again. He changed his position, thinking furiously. He hosed
bullets into the cracks.

A jeering cackle of laughter rattled through the slits.

"You allee same waste plenty bullet, do no good!" intoned
an Oriental voice.

With silence and speed, Renny slid out of his coat. He
bundled it about his right fist, making a thick pad. Guessing
where the iron rod would strike next, he held out his fist to
catch the blow. Three times, he failed. Then—*thud!*

The impact was terrific. He was slammed to the passage
end. The coat pad saved bones in his enormous fist from
breakage.

Slumping to the floor, Renny lay perfectly motionless.

REDDISH light spurted down through the cracks.

"The tiger sleeps," a man singsonged. "Seize him, my sons."

The rear passage door opened with little noise. A band of Mongols flung through and pounced upon Renny.

With an angry roar, Renny heaved up. He spun a complete circle, the machine-gun muzzle blowing a red flame from his big fist.

Yells, screams, gasps made a grisly bedlam. Bodies fell. Wounded men pitched about like beheaded chickens.

Renny hurtled out of the passage—and received a blow over the head from one of the iron rods. He sagged like a man stricken with deathly illness. He lost his gun.

He was buried by an avalanche of slant-eyed men. His wrists and ankles received numberless turns of wire-strong silk cord. A huge sponge was tamped between his jaws and cinched there with more silken line.

One man drove a toe into Renny's ribs.

"The tiger devil has slain three of our brothers!" he snarled. "For that, he should die slowly and in great pain. Perhaps with the death of a thousand cuts."

"You have not forgotten, oh lord, that the master wants this white man alive?" queried another.

"I have not forgotten. The master is wise. This man is friend to our great enemy, the bronze devil. Perhaps we can persuade the bronze one to bother us no more, lest we slay this friend."

These words were exchanged in their cackling lingo. Renny understood the language, and could speak it after a fashion. He was no little relieved. He had expected to be killed on the spot, probably with fiendish torture.

A large wooden packing case was now tumbled into the room. It was a shipping crate for a radio, and was marked with the name of an advertised set.

They shoved Renny into the box, packing excelsior around him tightly, so he could hardly stir. The lid was nailed on. Thin cracks admitted air enough for breathing.

At this point, a commotion arose out in front. A neighbor had heard the shots and screams of dying men, and had called a cop.

"Velly solly!" a half-caste Celestial told the officer smugly. "Ladio, him makee noises."

"A radio, huh?" grunted the policeman, not satisfied. "Reckon I'll take a look around, anyway."

In the rear of the establishment, Orientals worked swiftly. They removed the dead and wounded. They threw rugs over the bloodstained floor and hung draperies over the bullet-marked armor plate on the doors.

"Ladio makee noise," repeated the Oriental. "If you want takee look-see, all lightee."

The cop was conducted into the rear. He noted nothing peculiar about the passage—the slits in the ceiling had been closed. He saw two bland-looking, moonfaced men loading a large radio case onto a truck behind the store. The truck already bore other crates.

"Me show how ladio makee lacket," said the Celestial.

He turned on one of several radio sets which stood about. Obviously, it was not working properly. Loud scratchings and roarings poured from it. The voice of a woman reading cooking recipes was a procession of deafening squawks.

The cop was satisfied.

"Reckon that's what the party who called me heard," he grunted. "After this, don't turn that thing on so loud, see! I ain't got no time to go chasin' down false alarms."

The officer departed.

The proprietor of the radio store made sure the policeman was out of sight, then he padded back to the truck.

"Take our prisoner to the master, my sons," he commanded.

THE truck rumbled away. It mingled with traffic that jammed the narrow streets of Chinatown. The two Orientals sat stolidly in the cab. They did not look back once.

Eventually, the truck rolled into a large warehouse. The packing cases were all unloaded and shoved on a freight elevator. The cage lifted several floors.

Renny was having difficulty breathing. The excelsior had worked up around his nostrils. It scratched his eyes.

He felt himself being tumbled end over end across floor. He could barely hear his captors talking.

"Go and tell the master we are here," one said, speaking their native tongue.

An Oriental padded off. In three or four minutes, he was back.

With swift rendings, the lid was torn off Renny's prison. They hauled him out and plucked the excelsior away.

He was in a large storeroom. A few boxes of merchandise were scattered about. Judging from the tags, most of it was from the Orient. In addition to the elevator and a stairway door, there was an opening to the right.

A man grunting under the weight of Renny's shoulders, another bearing his feet, they passed through the opening. A flight of creaking stairs was ascended. A trapdoor lifted, letting them out on a tarred roof.

An unusually high wall concealed them from other buildings near by. Renny was carried over and flung across a narrow gap to the roof of the adjacent building. Next, he was carried to a large chimney.

Reaching into the flue, an Oriental brought out a rope. This was tied under Renny's arms. They lowered him. He saw the interior of the chimney was quite clean, fitted with a steel ladder.

He was handed down all of a hundred feet. Then half a dozen clawlike hands seized him and yanked him through an aperture in the chimney.

Renny gazed about in surprise.

His surroundings were luxurious. Expensive tapestries draped the walls; rugs, many more than an inch thick, strewed the floor. A low tabouret near one wall bore a steaming teapot, tiny cups and containers of melon seeds and other delicacies of the Far East.

Mongols and half-caste Chinese stood about. Each one was dressed neatly and might have been an American business man, except for their inscrutable faces and the hate blazing in their dark eyes. Renny counted seven of them.

Suddenly an eighth man appeared. He made a startling announcement.

"The master has received important news!" he singsonged. "News which makes it no longer necessary that we refrain from taking the life of this one who has hands the size of four ordinary men. He is to pay for slaying our fellows."

RENNY felt as if he had been shoved into a refrigerator. The Oriental's statement amounted to a pronouncement of death.

But it was more than that. It told Renny something terrible had happened. They had intended to hold him as a hostage to force Doc Savage to leave them alone. Now they no longer needed him for that. Had they succeeded in slaying Doc?

"This man is to be administered the death of many cuts," continued the slant-eyed man. "Four of you bring the other two prisoners here."

Obeying the order, four men departed. They came back almost at once bearing two bound and gagged figures.

Renny had no trouble guessing who they were.

Juan Mindoro and Scott S. Osborn!

Juan Mindoro was a slender, dynamic man. His high forehead and clear eyes gave him a distinctive look. Gray peppered his dark hair. A gray mustache bristled over his gag.

Scott S. Osborn, the sugar importer, was a guinea-pig fat man. Ordinarily, his hair was stuck down with grease, but now it was disarrayed and hung in thin strings. His eyes were bubbly and running tears.

The spokesman of the yellow horde slanted an arm at Scott S. Osborn. He spoke in snarling English.

Scott S. Osborn's fat body convulsed. Tears fairly squirted from his little, fat-encircled eyes. His scream of terror was a shrill whinny through his nostrils.

The Mongol wheeled on Mindoro.

"You will watch!" he grated. "As you watch, you will do well to think deeply, my fliend!"

Juan Mindoro only glowered back at his tormentor. No quiver of fear rippled his distinctive features.

"You have lefused to give us the names of the men in the seclet political society of the Luzon Union, which you head," continued the Mongol, only a few "R's" turned into "L's" marring his pronunciation of the English words. "We need those names."

Dropping to a knee, the slant-eyed man hastily removed Juan Mindoro's gag. "Maybe so, you give us the names now. In such case, we would see fit not to halm these two men."

"I am not fool enough to trust you!" Juan Mindoro said fiercely, speaking crisp, Americanized English. "You want the names of my friends in the secret political society so you can slay them and get them out of the way. They would all be assassinated."

"But, no," smirked the Mongol. "We would only lemove them fol a sholt time. Kidnap them, pelhaps."

"Kill them, you mean!" snapped Mindoro. "You won't get their names from me. That's final!" Then, looking at Renny, he added, as though to explain his action, "The information they want would mean the death of hundreds of innocent men. The decision I must make is a horrible one, for it means my death as well as your own. I think they will kill me within a few hours."

Renny shrugged—the only reply he could make.

Snarling, the Mongol pointed at Renny. "Begin! Cut out his eyes to stalt!"

A yellow man flashed a needle-bladed knife. He dropped on Renny, put his knee on Renny's chest, grasped the big man's hair with his left fist.

The knife lifted. Every eye in the room watched it.

A Mongol over by the entrance to the chimney shrieked. He shot like a living cannon ball across the room. He struck the knifeman with a shock that knocked them both unconscious.

Wild stares centered on the chimney entrance.

A giant man of bronze stood there!

Chapter 8

A PIRATE OF TO-DAY

FOR once, the yellow faces of the Mongols were not inscrutable. They goggled like small boys seeing their first lion.

"Fools!" ripped their leader. "Kill this bronze devil!"

A man darted a hand to his sleeve and forked out a kris with a foot-long serpentine blade. He drew back his arm and flung the knife.

What happened next was almost black magic. The kris was suddenly protruding from the chest of the man who had thrown it! It was as though he had stabbed himself.

Not one present could believe the mighty bronze man had plucked the flashing blade out of mid-air and returned it so accurately and with such blinding speed. No one, except Renny, who had seen Doc perform such amazing feats before!

Even while the dead man sloped backward to the floor like a falling tree, Doc seized another Mongol. The fellow seemed to become light as a rag doll, and as helpless. His clubbed body bowled over a fifth Oriental.

Only three were now left. One of these drew a revolver, flung it up, fired rapidly. But he did nothing, except drive bullets into the body of his fellow as it came hurtling toward him. The next instant, he was smashed down, to lose his senses when his head smacked the wall.

The surviving pair spun and fled with grotesque leaps. They squawked in terror at each jump.

They dived through a door, but retained presence of mind enough to slam and lock the panel.

Doc struck it, found it was of armor plate, and did not waste more time.

Whirling back, he scooped up a knife and cut through the bonds of the captives.

Renny was hardly on his feet before Doc had entered the chimney.

The hundred feet to the top, Doc climbed in almost no time. He ran across the roof.

Down in the street, the Orientals were piling into a sedan. The machine hooted up the thoroughfare, skidded around a corner, and was gone.

Doc knew any attempt to follow would be fruitless. He descended the chimney, joining the others.

"How'd you find us?" Renny wanted to know.

"Through the police," Doc explained. "They had been telephoning me news of every suspicious incident, however unimportant, in this part of town. I got word of the reported screams and shots in the radio store, and came to investigate. I heard the two truck drivers receive orders to take their prisoner to their boss. It was a simple matter to follow them here."

Doc now shook hands with Juan Mindoro.

DOC SAVAGE had once visited a number of islands in the Pacific, studying tropical fevers and their cures. It was on this trip that he had first met Juan Mindoro. The meeting had come about through a medical clinic which Mindoro maintained. Mindoro was extremely wealthy, expended tremendous sums on projects for the general benefit of humanity. The medical clinic, treating poor people without charge, was only one of the many philanthropies he indulged in.

Doc had been impressed with the high character of Juan Mindoro. So much so, indeed, that he had offered his services to Mindoro, should they ever be needed.

"It is hopeless for me to try to express my thanks to you with mere words," Juan Mindoro said, his orator's voice husky with emotion. "They would surely have killed me, those Mongol fiends."

Doc now turned to Scott S. Osborn. He was surprised when Osborn shrank away as if expecting a blow.

"You can't do anything to me!" Osborn shrieked hysterically. "I've got money! I'll fight you through every court in the land!"

Puzzled, Doc turned to Juan Mindoro. "What does he mean?"

Mindoro gave Osborn a scowl of scathing contempt.

"I came to this man, thinking he was my friend," he said. "He offered to hide me, and took me to his home. Then he went to my enemies. They paid him money to tell them where I was."

"But they captured him at the same time they took you," Doc pointed out. "And a moment ago, they were going to kill him."

Juan Mindoro's laugh was a dry rattle. "They double-crossed him. He was a fool. He thought they could be trusted."

Osborn wiped his bubbly eyes. His weak mouth made a trembling sneer.

"You can't do anything to me for selling you out!" he said shrilly. "My money will see to that! I've still got the dough they paid me for telling where you were, Mindoro! Fifty thousand dollars! I'll spend every cent of it to fight you in court!"

Mindoro suddenly picked up a gun one of the Mongols had dropped. He fingered it slowly, gazing all the while at Osborn.

"I wish I were less of a civilized man!" he said coldly. "I would shoot this dog!"

Doc reached up and got the gun. Mindoro gave it up readily.

"Osborn has been punished," Doc said grimly. "He became involved with the Mongols through his own greed. They murdered his brother last night. Had he not gone to them, that would never have happened."

Osborn's fat little face went starkly white. "What's this—this about my brother?"

"He was murdered last night."

This was obviously Osborn's first knowledge of his brother's slaughter. It hit him hard. He turned whiter and whiter until his repulsive little head became like a thing of bleached marble. He seemed hardly to breathe. Tears oozed from his small eyes, chased each other down his puffy cheeks, and wetted his shirt front and necktie.

"My own brother—I just the same as murdered him!" he choked in a voice so low the others hardly heard.

Ignoring him, Doc indicated the doorway into the chimney. "I suggest we get out of here."

They turned toward the chimney. Then Renny yelped excitedly and sprang for Osborn.

He was too late. Osborn, crazed by the grief of his brother's death, crumpled to the floor, his body falling upon the upturned blade held by one of the dead Mongols.

THE body of the fat little man executed a few spasmodic jerks before it became a spongy pile upon the floor.

Mindoro, gazing at the body religiously, said in solemn tones: "May I be forgiven for speaking to him so harshly. I did not know of his brother's murder."

"He had it coming!" grunted Renny, who was about as hard boiled as they came.

Doc Savage made no comment.

They climbed the chimney, crossed the roof tops, and descended to the street by the same route Renny had been carried into this room.

Doc telephoned the police a brief report of what had happened. He ended with the request: "Keep my connection with the affair secret from the newspapers."

"Of course, Mr. Savage!" said the police captain who was receiving the news. "But can you give us a description of the leader of this herd of Mongols and half-castes?"

Doc turned to Juan Mindoro. "Who is behind this mess?"

"A man known as Tom Too," replied Mindoro.

"Can you describe him?"

Mindoro shook his head. "I have never seen the man. He did not show himself to me, even when I was held prisoner."

"No description," Doc told the police official.

They rode uptown in a taxi. Doc remained outside on the running board for the first few blocks. Then, as the machine slowed for a traffic light, he dropped off.

Even as Renny and Mindoro started to bark excited questions, the giant bronze man vanished—lost himself in the crowd that swarmed the walks of Broadway.

Mindoro wiped his high forehead in some bewilderment.

"A remarkable man," he muttered.

Renny grinned. "That ain't saying the half of it!"

A couple of blocks farther on, Renny sobered abruptly.

"Holy cow!" he ejaculated. "I forgot to tell Doc something! And I dang well know it's important!"

"What!"

"When the Mongols first got me, they were going to keep me alive as a hostage to make Doc behave. Then they suddenly decided to kill me, remarking that something had occurred which made it no longer necessary to keep me alive. I thought at the time that maybe they had gotten Doc. But that couldn't have been it."

"Well?"

Renny knotted his enormous hands. "I wonder what made them decide to kill me!"

IT was fully an hour later when Doc Savage appeared at his eighty-sixth-floor skyscraper retreat.

Ham, Renny, and Mindoro were waiting for him. They were perspiring and excited.

Waving his sword cane, Ham yelled: "Doc! They've got Monk, Johnny, and Long Tom!"

A stranger watching Doc would not have dreamed the shock this news conveyed. The bronze face remained as devoid of expression as metal. No change came into his eyes that were like pools of flake gold.

"When?" he asked. His strange voice, although not lifted to speak the single word, carried with the quality of a great drum beat.

"We were all going to meet here about noon," Ham explained. "I stopped for a manicure and was late. When I arrived, there was a lot of excitement. Several of the Mongols had just herded Long Tom, Johnny, and Monk out at the point of guns. They rode off in waiting cars. Nobody as much as got the license number of the cars."

Renny beat his big fists together savagely—the sound they made was like steel blocks colliding.

"Blast it, Doc!" he said sorrowfully. "I knew something was wrong when the devils decided so suddenly to croak me. But I forgot to tell you——"

"I heard their sudden change of intention," Doc replied.

Renny looked vastly relieved. He had thought that his forgetfulness was responsible for half an hour's delay in Doc getting on the trail of the captors of the trio.

"Did you guess they had captured our three pals?"

"The suspicion occurred to me," Doc admitted. "It became certain when I dropped off the taxi and called the manager of this building."

"Then you've been on their trail!" Renny grinned. "Find anything?"

"Nothing."

Renny's sober face set in disconsolate lines. With the others, he followed Doc back into the office.

From a drawer, Doc took a box containing cigars—cigars so expensive and carefully made that each was in an individual vacuum container. He offered these to the others, then held a light. Doc never smoked himself.

There was tranquillity in the giant bronze man's manner, a sphinxlike calmness that had the effect of quieting Ham and Renny. Even Juan Mindoro was noticeably eased.

Doc's weird golden eyes came to rest on Juan Mindoro.

"The master of the Mongol horde is a man named Tom Too, and they are seeking to wipe out your secret political society in the Luzon Union," he said. "That is substantially all I know of this affair. Can you enlighten me further?"

"I certainly can!" Juan Mindoro clipped grimly. "This Tom Too is a plain pirate!"

"Pirate?"

"Exactly! A buccaneer compared to whom Captain Kidd, Blackbeard, and Sir Henry Morgan were petty thieves!"

Doc, Renny and Ham digested this. Renny had taken one of the cigars, although he rarely smoked. The weed looked like a brown toothpick in his enormous fist. Ham was leaning forward in an attitude of intense concentration, the sword cane supporting his hands under his jaw, his eyes staring at Mindoro.

"Tom Too got his start with the pirates of the China seaboard," Mindoro continued. "As you know, the China coast is the only part of the world where piracy still flourishes to any extent."

"Sure," Renny put in. "The steamers along the coast and on the rivers carry soldiers and machine guns. Even then, two to three hundred craft a year are looted."

"Tom Too became a power among the corsairs," Mindoro went on. "A year or two ago, he moved inland. He intended to set up an empire in the interior of China. He established himself as a war lord.

"But the armies of the Chinese republic drove him out. He moved into Manchuria and sought to seize territory and cities. But the Japanese were too much for him."

Renny twirled the cigar absently in his gigantic fingers. "This sounds a little fantastic."

"It is not fantastic—for the Orient," Doc Savage put in. "Many of the so-called war lords of the Far East are little better than pirates."

"Tom Too is the worst of the lot!" Mindoro interjected. "He is considered a devil incarnate, even in the Orient, where human life is held so very cheaply."

"You said you had never seen Tom Too," Doc suggested. "Yet you know a great deal concerning his career."

"What I am telling you is merely the talk of the cafés. It is common knowledge. Concrete facts about Tom Too are scarce. He keeps himself in the background. Yet his followers number into the hundreds of thousands."

"Huh?" Renny ejaculated.

"I told you the pirates of the Spanish Main were petty crooks compared to Tom Too!" Mindoro rapped. "It is certain no buccaneer of history ever contemplated a coup such as Tom Too plans. He is moving to seize the entire Luzon Union!"

"How much has he accomplished?" Doc asked sharply.

"A great deal. He has moved thousands of his men into the Luzon Union."

At this, Renny grunted explosively. "The newspapers have carried no word of such an invasion!"

"It has not been an armed invasion," Mindoro said grimly. "Tom Too is too smart for that. He knows foreign warships would take a hand.

"Tom Too's plan is much more subtle. He is placing his followers in the army and navy of the Luzon Union, in the police force, and elsewhere. Thousands of them are masquerading as merchants and laborers. When the time comes, they will seize power suddenly. There will be what the newspapers call a bloodless revolution.

"Tom Too will establish what will seem to the rest of the world to be a legitimate government. But every governmental position will be held by his men. Systematic looting will follow. They will take over the banks of the Union, the sugar plantations—the entire wealth of the republic."

"Where do you come in on this?" Renny wanted to know.

Mindoro made a savage gesture. "Myself and my secret political organization are all that stands in the way of Tom Too!"

Chapter 9

HIS ARM FELL OFF

HAM had said nothing throughout the discussion. He maintained his attitude of intense concentration. Ham was a good listener on occasions such as this. His keen brain had a remarkable capacity for grasping details and formulating courses of action.

"Have you taken this matter up with the larger nations?" Ham asked now.

Mindoro nodded. "That was my first move."

"Didn't you get any action?"

"A lot of vague diplomatic talk was all!" Mindoro replied. "They told me in so many words that they thought I exaggerated the situation."

"Then no one will interfere, even if Tom Too seizes power with this bloodless revolution he plans," Doc said. His words were a statement of fact.

Tilting back in his char, Doc drew his sleeve off his left wrist.

Mindoro stared curiously at the contrivance that looked like an overgrown wrist watch. He did not know the thing was the scanning lens of Doc's amazingly compact television receiver. He seemed about to ask what it was, but the gravity of his own troubles dissuaded him temporarily.

"I will describe my secret political organization briefly, and show how we are fighting Tom Too," Mindoro stated. "In the secret group are most of the prominent men of the Luzon Union, including the president, his cabinet and the more important officials. We have money and power. We control the newspapers. We have the confidence of the people.

"Most important of all, we are sufficient in number to take up arms and offer Tom Too very stiff opposition. We already have the very latest in machine guns and airplanes. We stand ready to fight the instant Tom Too comes into the open.

"Tom Too has learned this. That alone is forcing him to postpone his coup. He is seeking to learn our identity. He captured me here in New York and tried to force me to reveal the names of the secret society members. Once in possession of those names, he will remove every man. Then he will seize power."

Doc put a hand inside his coat, where he wore the receiving apparatus of his television receptor. A faint click sounded. He glanced at his wrist.

A molten glow came into his golden eyes, a strange, hot luminance.

"Isn't there something you can do toward rescuing your three friends?" Mindoro asked Doc.

"I'm doing it now," Doc told him.

Mindoro was puzzled. "I don't understand."

"Come here and look." Doc indicated the disk on his wrist.

The others leaped to his side.

"Holy cow!" Renny shouted out. "Why, there's Long Tom, Monk, and Johnny!"

FLICKERING on the crystal-like lense of the telewatch was the somewhat vague image of a dingy office interior. The place held a pair of desks, filing cabinets, and worn chairs.

On three of the chairs sat Long Tom, Monk, and Johnny. They were bound hand and foot, tied to the chairs, and gagged.

"I know that place," Renny ejaculated. "It's the office of the Dragon Oriental Goods Company, across the street from the skyscraper under construction."

"Our friends were just brought in," said Doc.

Mindoro made bewildered gestures.

"That is a television instrument, of course," he muttered. "But I did not know they were made that small."

"They're not, usually," Doc explained. "But this one is not radically different from the larger sets. It is merely reduced in size. Being so small, it is effective for only a few miles."

"Where is the transmitter?" Renny questioned. "In the Dragon joint?"

"In the adjoining office. I installed it after leaving you and Mindoro in the taxi. Other transmitters, operating on slightly different wave lengths, are at the radio store and at the spot where Tom Too so nearly finished you. This one got results first."

Ham ran into the laboratory. He came out bearing several of the compact little machine guns which were Doc's own invention, gas masks, gas bombs, and bullet-proof vests.

Riding down in the high-speed elevator, Ham, Renny, and Mindoro donned the vests, belted on the machine guns, and stuffed their pockets with bombs.

Mindoro, who was unfamiliar with Doc's working methods, showed astonishment that the mighty bronze man did not follow their example.

"Aren't you going to carry at least one of these guns?" he queried.

Doc's bronze head shook a negative. "Rarely use them."

"But why?"

Doc was slow answering. He didn't like to talk about himself or his way of operating.

"The reasons I don't use a gun are largely psychological," he said. "Put a gun in a man's hand, and he will use it. Let him carry one and he comes to depend upon it. Take it away from him, and he is lost—seized with a feeling of helplessness. Therefore, since I carry no firearms, none can be taken from me to leave the resultant feeling of helplessness."

"But think of the handicap of not being armed!" Mindoro objected.

Doc shrugged and dropped the subject.

Ham and Renny grinned at this word play.

Doc handicapped? Not much! They had never seen the mighty bronze man in a spot yet where he didn't have a ready way out.

Doc rode the outside of the cab which whisked them down Broadway. He watched the diallike lens of his telewatch almost continuously.

Several Mongols were now in the Dragon concern office. They moved about, conversing. The image carried to Doc by television was too jittery and dim to permit him to read their lips. Indeed, he could not even identify the faces of the men in the room, beyond the fact that they were lemon-hued and slant-eyed.

Considering the compactness of Doc's tiny apparatus, however, the transmitted image was remarkably clear. An electrical engineer interested in television would have gone into raptures over the mechanism. It was constructed with the precision of a lady's costly wrist watch.

An interesting bit of drama was now enacted on the telewatch lens.

Monk, by squirming about in the chair in which he was bound, got his toes on the floor. Hopping like a grotesque, half-paralyzed frog, he suddenly reached the grimy window. He fell against the pane. It broke.

Some glass fell inside the room; some dropped down into the street.

A yellow man ran to Monk and delivered a terrific blow. Monk upset, chair and all, onto the floor. He landed on fragments of the window he had broken. Doc watched Monk's hands intently after the fall.

The Mongols peered anxiously out of the window. They drew back after a time, satisfied the falling glass had alarmed no one.

Doc's view was now interrupted.

A slant-eyed man came and stood directly before the eye of the hidden television transmitter. All the apparatus registered was a limited view of the fellow's back.

Doc waited, golden eyes never leaving the telewatch dial. None of his impatience showed on his bronze features. Three minutes passed. Four. Then the Mongol moved away from the television eye.

The situation in the Dragon concern office was exactly as it had been four minutes ago. The three forms bound to chairs were quiet.

Doc's head shook slowly.

"I don't like this," he told those inside the taxi. "Something strange is happening in that office."

Doc continued to watch the scanning lens. The three tied to the chairs were motionless as dead men. He could not see their faces.

"We're almost there, Doc," Renny said from the cab interior.

Doc directed the driver to stop the machine. They got out.

"Let's rush 'em!" Renny suggested, his voice a rumble like thunder in a barrel.

"That is probably what they're hoping we'll do," Doc told him dryly.

Renny started. "You think this is a trick?"

"Tom Too is clever enough to know you picked up the trail of his man at the Dragon concern office. He must surely know we are aware he has been using the office. Yet he chanced discovery in bringing our pals there, or having his men bring them. He would not do that without a reason."

"But what——"

"Wait here!"

Leaving them behind, Doc moved down a side street. Two or three pedestrians turned to stare after his striking figure, startled by sight of a physique such as they had not glimpsed before.

SOME distance down the side street, a street huckster stood beside a two-wheeled hand cart piled high with apples and oranges. This man had but recently arrived from his native land in the south of Europe, and he spoke little English.

He was surprised when a voice hailed him in his native tongue. He was impressed by the appearance of the bronze, golden-eyed man who had accosted him. A short conversation ensued. Some money changed hands.

The huckster wheeled his cart to a secluded spot. But he shortly reappeared, pushing his vehicle toward Broadway. He turned south on Broadway, and was soon before the Far East Building, on the tenth floor of which was the office of the Dragon Oriental Goods Company.

The door of the Far East Building was wide. The huckster calmly wheeled his car inside an unheard-of thing.

The half-caste elevator operator dashed forward angrily. Another man was loitering in the lobby. His broad face, prominent cheek bones and almost entire absence of beard denoted, to an expert observer, Mongol blood. He joined the elevator operator.

They proceeded to throw the fruit vender out bodily. It took both of them. They wrestled the peddler clear to the sidewalk and dumped him into the gutter. Then they came back and shoved the cart out.

Neither man noticed the fruit in the cart was not heaped as high as it had been a moment before.

The huckster wheeled his vehicle away, barking excitedly in his native tongue. He disappeared.

Doc Savage had been hidden under the fruit. No one but the peddler knew Doc was now in the Far East Building— least of all the Mongol in the lobby, who was obviously one of Tom Too's pirate horde.

"Me think that velly stlange thing to happen," the Mongol told the elevator operator.

"Allee same lookee funny," agreed the operator. "Mebbe so that fella wolk alongside blonze man?"

The Mongol swore a cackling burst in his native tongue. "Me thinkee good thing follow fluit fella! Alee same cut thloat and play safe."

With this, he felt a knife inside his sleeve and started out. He reached the door.

Splat! The sound was dull, mushy. It came from the side of the door. Thin glass fragments of a hollow ball tinkled on the floor tiling.

The Mongol went to sleep on his feet—fell without a sound.

Doc had hurled one of his anæsthetic balls from the stairway. He had not intended to reveal his presence. But it was necessary that he protect the innocent huckster whom he had bribed to bring him here.

The elevator operator spun. He saw Doc. A screech of fright split past his lips. He charged wildly for the street door.

The cloud of invisible, odorless anæsthetic had not yet become ineffective. The man ran into it. He folded down, and momentum tumbled him head over heels across the walk.

Doc stepped to the door.

From two points—one up the street, one down it— machine guns brayed a loud stream of reports.

Doc had expected something like that. This was a trap, and Tom Too's men were hardly fools enough to wait for him on the upper floors of the building, where their retreat would be cut off.

He flashed backward in time to get in the clear.

Fistfuls of stone powdered off the building entrance as jacketed bullets stormed. Falling glass jangled loudly. Ricocheting lead squawled in the lobby.

Doc glided to the stairs, mounted to the second floor and tried the door of a front office. It chanced to be locked. He pulled—not overly hard, it seemed. The lock burst from its anchorage as though hitched to a tractor.

Entering the office, Doc crossed to a window and glanced down.

The machine guns had silenced. A gray sedan sped along the street, slowing to permit the Mongols to dive aboard. The car continued north. It reached the first corner.

Suddenly there was a series of sawing sounds, like the rasp of a gigantic bull fiddle.

Doc knew those noises instantly—the terrific fire of the compact little machine guns he had invented. Renny, Ham, and Mindoro had turned loose on the Orientals.

The gray sedan careened to the left. It hurdled the curb. There was a roar of rent wood and smashing glass as it hit a display window. The car passed entirely through the window. Wheels ripped off, fenders crumpled, top partially smashed in, it sledded across the floor of a furniture store.

Doc saw the attackers wade through the wreckage after the car. Several times their little machine guns made the awful bull-fiddle sawings.

Then the three men came out and sped toward the Far East Building.

Doc met them downstairs.

"Three of the devils were in the car!" Renny grimaced. "They're all ready for the morgue."

"What about our pals?" Ham demanded. He seized Doc's wrist and stared at the telewatch dial. "Good! They're still tied to those chairs!"

Doc said nothing. His golden eyes showed no elation.

They rode up in the elevator. Renny raced down the tenth-floor corridor. He did not wait to see whether the Dragon concern office door was locked. His keg of a fist whipped a terrific blow. The stout panel jumped out of the frame like match wood.

Renny, continuing forward, tore the door from its hinges with his great weight.

Ham leaped to one of the bound figures, grasped it by the arm. Then he emitted a squawk of horror.

The arm of the form had come off in his hand!

"THEY'RE dummies," Doc said. "The clothes worn by Monk, Long Tom, and Johnny—stuffed with waste paper, and fitted with the faces of show-window dummies."

Ham shuddered violently. "But we saw Monk, Long Tom, and Johnny in here! They were moving about, or at least struggling against their bonds."

"They were here," Doc admitted. "But they were taken away and the dummies substituted while one of the Mongols stood in front of the television transmitter, unless I'm mistaken."

Renny's sober face was black with gloom. "Then they knew the television sender was installed here!"

"They were lucky enough to find it," Doc agreed. "So they brought the three prisoners here, hoping we would see them and come to the rescue. They had the machine-gun trap down in the street waiting for us. That explains the whole thing."

Ham made a slashing gesture with his sword cane. "Blast it! We haven't accomplished anything!"

Doc swung over to the fragments of broken window lying on the floor. One piece was about a foot square, the others smaller. He began gathering them.

"What possible value can that glass have?" Mindoro questioned curiously, still trembling a little from the excitement of the recent fight.

"Monk broke this window and his captors knocked him over," Doc replied. "He lay on top of the glass fragments for a time, while the Mongols looked down at the window to see if the breaking window had caused alarm. They did not watch Monk at all for a few seconds. During that time, I distinctly saw Monk work a crayon of the invisible-writing chalk out of his pocket and write something on the glass."

Renny lumbered for the door. "The ultra-violet apparatus is at the office. We'll have to take the glass there."

They left the Far East Building by a rear door, thus avoiding delay while explanations were being furnished the police.

In Doc's eighty-sixth-floor retreat, they put the glass fragments under the ultra-violet lamp.

Monk's message confronted them, an unearthly bluish scrawl. It was brief, but all-important.

Tom Too is scared and taking a run-out powder. He is going to Frisco by plane and sailing for the Luzon Union on the liner *Malay Queen*. He's taking us three along as hostages to keep you off his neck. Give 'im hell, Doc!

"Good old Monk!" Ham grinned. "That homely ape does pull a fast one once in a while. He's heard the gang talking among themselves. Probably they figured he couldn't understand their lingo."

Mindoro had paled visibly. He strained his graying hair through palsied fingers.

"This means bloodshed!" he muttered thickly. "Tom Too has given up trying to get the roster of my political group. He will strike, and my associates will fight him. Many will die."

Doc Savage scooped up the phone. He gave a number—that of a Long Island airport.

"My plane!" he said crisply. "Have it ready in an hour."

"You think we can overhaul them from the air?" Ham demanded.

"Too risky for our three pals," Doc pointed out.

"Then what——"

"We're going to be on the liner *Malay Queen* when she sails from Frisco!"

Chapter 10

THE LUZON TRAIL

THE liner *Malay Queen*, steaming out through the Golden Gate, was an impressive sight. No doubt many persons on the San Francisco water front paused to admire the majesty of the vessel. She was a bit over seven hundred feet long. In shipbuilding parlance, she displaced thirty thousand tons.

The hull was black, with a strip of red near the water line; the superstructure was a striking white. The craft had been built when everybody had plenty of money to spend. All the luxuries had been put into her—swimming pool, three dining saloons, two lounges, two smoking rooms, writing room, library, and two bars. She even carried a small bank.

Most of the passengers were on deck, getting their last look at the Golden Gate. At Fort Point and Fort Baker, the nearest points of land on either side, construction work on the new Golden Gate bridge was in evidence—a structure which would be nearly six and a half thousand feet in length when completed.

Among the passengers were some strange personages.

Of exotic appearance, and smacking of the mystery of the Orient, was the Hindu who stood on the boat deck. Voluminous white robes swathed this man from neck to ankles. Occasionally the breeze blew back his robes to disclose the brocaded sandals he wore. A jewel flamed in his ample turban.

Such of his hair as was visible had a jet-black color. His brown face was plump and well-fed. Under one ear, and reaching beneath his chin to his other ear, was a horrible scar. It looked as though somebody had once tried to cut the Hindu's throat. He wore dark glasses.

Even more striking was the Hindu's gigantic black servant. This fellow wore baggy pantaloons, a flamboyant silk sash, and sandals which had toes that curled up and over. On each turned-over toe was a tiny silver bell.

This black man wore no shirt, but made up for it with a barrel-sized turban. He had thick lips, and nostrils which flared like those of a hard-running horse.

Passengers on the *Malay Queen* had already noted that the Hindu and his black man were never far apart.

"A pair of bloomin' tough-lookin' blokes, if yer asks me," remarked a flashy cockney fellow, pointing at the Hindu and the black. "Hi'd bloody well 'ate to face 'em in a dark alley. Yer'd better lock up them glass marbles yer wearin', dearie."

The cockney had addressed a stiff-backed, very fat dowager in this familiar fashion. They were perfect strangers. The dowager gave the cockney a look that would have made an Eskimo shiver.

"Sir!" she said bitingly, then flounced off.

The cockney leered after her. He was dressed in the height of bad taste. The checks in his suit were big and loud; his tie and shirt were violently colored. He wore low-cut shoes that were neither tan nor black, but a bilious red hue. His hat was green. He smoked bad-smelling cigars, and was not in the least careful where he knocked his ashes. His face bore an unnatural paleness, as though he might have recently served a long prison term.

The cockney did not glance again at the Hindu and the black man.

The Hindu was Doc Savage. The black man was Renny. The cockney, he of the loud clothes and bad manners, was Ham—Ham, the one usually so immaculately clad and so debonair of manner. The disguises were perfect, a tribute to Doc's intensive study of the make-up art.

Down on the promenade deck, a steward was confronting one of the steerage passengers who had wandered into territory reserved for those traveling first class.

"You'll have to get back down where you belong!" growled the steward, showing scant politeness.

Courtesy did not seem to be due such a character as the steerage passenger. The man was shabby, disheveled. In age he seemed to be less than thirty. But he looked like a fever-ridden tropical tramp. His skin was light in hue, and he was a pronounced blond.

A close observer might have noted his eyes were unusually dark for one so fair-complected.

This man was Juan Mindoro.

Shortly afterward, Mindoro sought to reach the upper decks again. This time he succeeded. He made his way furtively to the royal suite, the finest aboard. This was occupied by Doc and Renny—otherwise the Hindu and his black servant.

Mindoro unlocked the royal suite with a key Doc had furnished, entered, and wrote briefly on the bathroom mirror with a bit of crayonlike substance he produced from a pocket. He wrote near the top.

No stewards encountered the blowsy-looking tropical tramp as he returned to the steerage.

Fifteen minutes after this incident, Ham also entered the royal suite and left a message—written near the bottom of the mirror.

The *Malay Queen* was some miles out to sea before the Hindu and his black man stalked with great dignity to their royal suite and locked themselves in.

Doc turned the ultra-violet lamp on the bathroom mirror.

Mindoro's message read:

The steerage is full of half-castes, Chinese, Japanese, Malays, and Mongols. But I have seen nothing to show Tom Too is aboard.

Ham's communication was:

No sign of Monk, Long Tom, or Johnny. And how I hate these clothes!

Renny snorted at the reflection of his own black face in the mirror. "Ham sure cuts a swath in his green hat and blood-colored shoes. I'll bet he breaks the mirror in his cabin so he can't see himself."

Doc took off his turban. He had dyed his hair an extreme black.

"Did you see any sign of Tom Too or his prisoners, Renny?"

"Not a hair." Renny drew funnel-like flaring tubes from his nostrils.

"They came from New York to San Francisco by plane, we know. We located the aircraft they had chartered. And the pilots told us they had three prisoners along."

"The big point is—did they sail on the *Malay Queen?*"

"We have no proof they did. But Monk's message indicated they intended to."

Renny scowled at his sepia reflection in the mirror, apparently trying to see how fierce he could look. The result was a countenance utterly villainous, especially when he replaced the tubes which enlarged his nostrils.

"Holy cow!" he grunted. "I wouldn't even know myself! I don't think Tom Too will recognize us, Doc. That gives us a few days in which to work. That's a long time."

"We may need it. This Tom Too is as clever a devil as we've ever gone up against."

They were not long in learning just how true Doc's statement was.

HAM gave Doc Savage news of the first development. This occurred the following day.

Ham furnished Doc his information in a rather curious fashion. He did it by smoking his vile cigar. He was seated at one end of the lounge. Doc was ostensibly reading a book at the other.

Ham released short and long puffs of smoke from his lips. The short puffs were dots, the long ones dashes. Using them, Ham spelled out a sentence.

Have you heard the talk going over the ship about the three maniacs confined to a stateroom on D deck?

Tom Too or any of his men, were they in the lounge, would hardly have dreamed the silly-looking cockney was transmitting a message. And Tom Too might very well be present—quite a few Orientals were numbered among the first-class passengers sitting in the lounge.

Doc shook a negative with his head, making it seem he

was mentally disagreeing with something he had read in his book.

The three madmen are in Stateroom Sixty-six. Ham continued his smoke transmission. *Two Mongols are always on guard outside the cabin. Thats all I've been able to find out.*

"And that's plenty," muttered Renny, who had also spelled out Ham's smoke words.

Shortly after this the Hindu and his giant black servant retired to their royal suite.

"That means they've got our buddies prisoners in the cabin!" Renny declared. "They've given out the word they're madmen to explain their keeping out of sight. Probably they're strapped in strait-jackets, and gagged, too."

Doc nodded grimly. "You stay here, Renny. I'm going down and investigate—alone."

For the first time, passengers on the *Malay Queen* saw the exotic-looking Hindu moving about without his black man. Several eyes followed him as he entered the elevator.

"I wish to be let out on D deck," he told the elevator man, speaking the precise English of one to whom the tongue is not native.

D deck, being the lowest on the ship, held the cheapest accommodations. The staterooms were not perfectly ventilated, and it was necessary to keep the ports of the outside cabins closed much of the time lest waves slosh in and cause damage.

Cabin No. 66 was far forward.

Sure enough, two slant-eyed fellows lounged before the door. These were not half-castes, but of pure Mongol strain. Both of them looked fairly intelligent.

Blank-eyed, they watched the robed Hindu approach. With each step the Hindu's rich sandals appeared under his robes. He came to a stop within arm reach of the two Mongols.

What followed next was forever a mystery to the Mongol pair.

Two sharp cracks sounded. Each man dropped.

Doc had struck with both fists simultaneously, before either victim realized what he intended to do. Indeed, neither Mongol as much as saw Doc's white-swathed arms start their movement.

The stateroom door was locked. Doc exerted pressure. The door caved in. Doc glided warily through.

The stateroom was empty!

Doc was not given long to digest this disappointing discovery. Two shots crashed in the passage outside. They came close together, deafening roars.

Doc whipped over to a berth, scooped up a pillow, and flashed it briefly outside the door. More shots thundered. Bullets tore a cloud of feathers out of the pillow.

With a gesture too quick for watching eyes to catch, Doc flicked a glass ball of anæsthetic into the passage.

He held his breath a full four minutes—not a difficult task, considering Doc had practiced doing that very thing every day of his life since he had quitted the cradle.

In the interim he heard excited shouts. Men ran up. But their shouts ceased and they fell unconscious as the gas got them.

When he knew the anæsthetic vapor had become ineffective, Doc stepped out.

Only stewards and ship officers lay senseless in the passage. Of the man who had fired the shots there was no sign.

Both of the Mongols had bullet holes through their brains.

For the moment no other observers were in sight. Doc hurried past the unconscious sailors and returned to the royal suite.

Renny was disappointed when Doc appeared without their three friends.

"What did you find?" he demanded.

"That Tom Too is about as clever a snake as ever lived!" Doc replied grimly.

"What'd he do?"

"Spread a false story about three madmen being in the cabin just on the chance I was aboard. He figured that if I was, I'd investigate. Well, I accommodated him. And now he knows who I am."

"A bad break!" Renny growled.

"Tom Too is an utterly cold-blooded killer. He sacrificed two of his men, murdering them just so they would not fall into my hands. No doubt he feared they would be scared into betraying him."

Renny jerked a cast of dental composition out of his mouth. It was this which had thickened his lips.

"No need of us wearing these disguises any longer!" he declared.

"No," Doc agreed. "They'd just make us that much easier to find. Ham and Mindoro are safe for the time being in their disguises, though."

The two men busied themselves shedding their make-up.

Remover used by theatrical players took the stain off their skin and hair. Doc peeled his throat scar off as though it were adhesive tape.

"This puts us in a tough spot," Renny rumbled as they returned themselves to normal appearance. "They'll spare no effort to put us out of the way. And no telling how many of them are aboard."

It was a vastly different-looking pair of men who stepped out of the royal suite. They were so changed an approaching deck steward did not recognize them.

"Is the Hindu in?" questioned the steward. "I got a note for him."

Doc plucked the note out of the startled steward's fingers.

It read:

There is an ancient saying about the straw that broke the back of the camel. Your next move will be the straw needed to break my patience.

Your three friends are alive and well—as long as my patience remains intact.

TOM TOO.

"The brass of the guy!" gritted Renny.

"Who gave you this?" Doc demanded of the steward.

"I dunno," muttered the flunky. "I was walkin' along, an it dropped at my feet. There was a five-dollar bill clipped to it, together with a note askin' me to deliver it. Somebody must 'a' throwed it."

Doc's golden eyes bored into those of the steward until he was convinced the man spoke the truth.

"On what deck did that happen?"

"On this one."

Chapter 11

PERIL LINER

MORE questioning revealed that no one had been in sight when the steward looked around after having the note dropped at his feet.

The steward departed; perspiring a little. That night he didn't sleep well, what with dreaming of uncanny golden eyes which had seemed to suck the truth out of him like magnets pulling at steel bars.

In the royal suite, Renny made grim preparations. He donned a bullet-proof vest and harnessed two of Doc's compact machine guns under his arms, where they wouldn't bulge his coat too much.

"Tom Too is not gonna set back and wait to see if we intend to lay off him," he rumbled wrathfully. "We've got to watch our step."

"Not a bad idea," Doc agreed. "From now on we take no more meals in the dining saloon."

"I hope we ain't gonna fast," grunted Renny, who was a heavy eater.

"Concentrated rations are in our baggage."

"Any chance of a prowler poisoning the stuff?"

"Very little. It would be next to impossible to get into the containers without breaking the seals."

Renny completed his grim preparations. He straightened his coat, then surveyed himself in the mirror. His garments had been tailored to conceal guns worn in under-arm holsters. The bullet-proof vest was inside, worn as an undergarment. Renny did not look like a walking fortress.

"What are we going to do about Tom Too?" he asked.

"We'll move slowly, for the time being. We don't want to get him excited enough to kill our pals," Doc said. "Our first move will be to consult the captain of the ship."

They found Captain Hickman, commander of the *Malay Queen*, on his bridge.

Captain Hickman was a short-legged man with a body that was nearly egg-shaped. Sea gales and blistering tropical suns had reddened his face until it looked as if it had been soaked in beet juice. His uniform was resplendent with gold braid and brass buttons.

Four nattily clad apprentice officers stood on the bridge, keeping watch over the instruments.

The first mate strode sprucely back and forth, supervising the apprentices and the general operation of the liner.

The first mate was somewhat of a fashion plate, his uniform being impeccable. He was a slender, pliant man with good shoulders and a thin-featured, not unhandsome face. His skin had a deeply tanned hue. His eyes were elevated a trifle at the outer corners, lending a suspicion some of his ancestors had been Orientals. This was not unusual, considering the *Malay Queen* plied the Orient trade.

Doc introduced himself to Captain Hickman.

"Savage—Savage—hm-m-m!" Captain Hickman murmured, stroking his red jaw. "Your name sounds very familiar, but I can't quite place it."

The first mate came over, saying: "No doubt you saw this man's name in the newspapers, captain. Doc Savage conducted the mysterious submarine expedition to the arctic regions. The papers were full of it."

"To be sure!" ejaculated Captain Hickman. Then he introduced the first mate. "This is Mr. Jong, my first officer."

The impeccable first mate bowed, his polite smile increasing the Oriental aspect of his features to a marked degree.

Doc Savage and Renny went into consultation with Captain Hickman in the latter's private sitting room.

"We have reason to believe three of my friends are being held prisoner somewhere aboard this liner," Doc explained bluntly. "It is a human impossibility for two men, or even three or four, to search a boat this size. The captives could easily be shifted to a portion of the vessel which we had already searched, and we would be none the wiser. We therefore wish the aid of your crew, such of them as you trust implicitly."

Captain Hickman rubbed his brow. He seemed too surprised for words.

"It is extremely important the search be conducted with the utmost secrecy," Doc continued. "Any alarm will mean the death of my friends."

"This is highly irregular!" the commander objected.

"Possibly."

"Have you any authority to command such a search?"

The flaky gold in Doc's eyes began to take on a molten aspect, an indication of anger.

"I had hoped you would coöperate freely in this matter." No wrath was apparent in his powerful voice.

At this point a radio operator entered the cabin, saluted briskly, and presented Captain Hickman a message.

The florid commander read it. His lips compressed; his eyes hardened.

"No search of this ship will be made!" he snapped. "And you two men are under arrest!"

Renny sprang to his feet, roaring: "What're you trying to pull on us?"

"Calm down," Doc told him mildly. Then he asked Captain Hickman: "May I see that radiogram?"

The skipper of the *Malay Queen* hesitated, then passed the wireless missive over. It read:

CAPTAIN HICKMAN
COMMANDER S S *MALAY QUEEN*

SEARCH YOUR SHIP FOR MEN NAMED CLARK
SAVAGE JR ALIAS DOC SAVAGE AND COLONEL
JOHN RENWICK ALIAS RENNY RENWICK STOP AR-
REST BOTH AND HOLD STOP WANTED FOR MUR-
DERING SEVERAL MONGOLIANS AND CHINESE IN
NEW YORK CITY STOP SAN FRANCISCO POLICE
DEPARTMENT

"Holy cow!" Renny thundered his pet expletive. "How did
they know we were aboard?"

"They didn't," Doc said grimly. "This is Tom Too's work.
Call that radio operator in here, captain. We'll see if he
really received such a message."

"I'll do nothing of the sort!" snapped Captain Hickman.
"You two are under arrest."

With this statement the florid skipper wrenched open a
drawer of his desk. He grasped a revolver reposing there.

Doc's bronze hand floated out and came to rest on Captain
Hickman's right elbow. Tightening, the corded bronze digits
seemed to bury themselves in the florid man's flesh.

Captain Hickman's fingers splayed open and let the gun
drop. He spat a stifled cry of pain.

Renny scooped up the fallen weapon.

Jong, the first mate, pitched into the sitting room, drawn
by his skipper's cry. Renny let Jong look into the noisy end of
the revolver, saying: "I wouldn't start anything, mister!"

Doc released Captain Hickman's elbow. The skipper dou-
bled over, whining with agony, nursing his hurt elbow against
his egg of a stomach. At the same time he goggled at Doc's
metallic hand, as though unable to believe human fingers
could have hurt him so.

Jong stood with hands half uplifted, saying nothing.

"We'll go interview the radio operator," Doc declared.

THE radio installation on the *Malay Queen* consisted of a
large lobby equipped with a counter, where messages were
accepted, and two inner rooms holding enormous banks of
apparatus.

"The message was genuine, all right!" insisted the radio
operator. He gave the call letters of the San Francisco station
which had transmitted the missive.

Seating himself at the semiautomatic "bug" which served
in lieu of a sending key, Doc called the shore station and
verified this fact.

"Let's see your file of sent messages!" Doc directed the
operator.

A brief search turned up one which had been "marked off" as sent not more than twenty minutes ago. It was in code, the words meaningless.

"Who filed this?"

"I don't know," insisted the radio man. "I discovered it lying on the counter, together with the payment for transmission and a swell tip. Some one came in and left it without being observed."

"This Tom Too must be half ghost!" Renny muttered. He still held the captain's revolver, although neither the skipper of the *Malay Queen* nor First Mate Jong were offering resistance.

Doc studied the cipher message. It read:

JOHN DUCK
HOTEL KWANG SAN FRANCISCO
   DTOSS EARVR AAGSE IAHBR OOAFR ODIRDA

There was no signature. Radiograms are often unsigned, which made this fact nothing unusual.

"Whew!" Renny grunted. "Can you make heads or tails of that mess of letters, Doc? It seems to be a five-letter code of some kind."

"The last word has six letters," Doc pointed out. "Let's see what a little experimenting will do to it."

Seating himself before a sheet of blank paper, a pencil in hand, Doc went to work on the cipher. His pencil flew swiftly, trying different combinations of the letters.

Five minutes later he got it.

"The thing is simple, after all," he smiled.

"Yeah?" Renny grunted doubtfully.

"The first cipher letter is the first in the translated message," Doc said rapidly. "The second cipher letter is the last in the message. The third cipher letter is the second in the message; the fourth cipher letter is next to the last in the message, and so on. The letters are merely scrambled systematically!"

"Hey!" gasped Renny. "I'm dizzy already."

"It sounds complicated until you get it down on paper Here, I'll show you."

Doc put down the cipher as it stood.

   DTOSS EARVR AAGSE IAHBR OOAFR ODIRDA

Under that he wrote the translation.

DOCSAVAGEABOARDRADIOFORHISARREST

Renny scowled at this. Then its meaning became clear—the words were merely without spacing.

"Doc Savage aboard. Radio for his arrest!" he read aloud.

"The instructions Tom Too sent to a confederate in San Francisco," Doc explained. "Evidently they had agreed upon a course of action should we be discovered aboard."

POWERFUL radio-telephone equipment was a part of the installation aboard the *Malay Queen*. Using this, it was possible for passengers aboard to carry on a telephone conversation with any one ashore, exactly as though there was a wire connection.

Using this, Doc now proceeded to do some detective work.

He called the Hotel Kwang in San Francisco.

"Have you a guest registered under the name of John Duck?" he asked.

"John Duck checked out only a few moments ago," the hotel clerk informed him.

Doc's second call was to the San Francisco police chief. He cut in a loud-speaker so every one in the *Malay Queen* radio room could hear what the police chief had to say.

"Have you received any request to arrest Doc Savage," Doc asked.

"Certainly not!" replied the San Francisco official. "We have a suggestion from the New York police that we offer Savage every possible coöperation."

Doc rested his golden eyes on Captain Hickman. "You satisfied?"

Captain Hickman's ruddy face glistened with perspiration. "I—er—yes, of course."

Doc severed his radio connection with San Francisco.

"I wish your coöperation," he told Captain Hickman. "Whether you give it or not is up to you. But if you refuse, you may rest assured you will lose your command of this ship within thirty minutes."

Captain Hickman mopped at his face. He was bewildered, angry, a little scared.

Doc noted his indecision. "Call your owners. Ask them about it."

The *Malay Queen* commander hurriedly complied. He secured a radio-land-line connection with the headquarters of his company in San Francisco. He gave a brief description of the situation.

"What about this man Savage?" he finished.

He was wearing earphones. The others did not hear what he was told.

But Captain Hickman turned about as pale as his ruddy face permitted. His hands shook as he placed the headset on the table. He stared at Doc as if wondering what manner of man the big bronze fellow was.

"I have been ordered to do anything you wish, even to turning my command over to you," he said briskly.

First Mate Jong stared as if this was hard to believe. Then he made a gesture of agreement. "I will start an immediate search of the ship. And I can promise you it will be done so smoothly no one will as much as know it is going on."

He hurried out.

Doc and Renny returned to the royal suite.

Renny eyed Doc curiously. "Just what kind of a pull have you got with the company that owns this boat, anyhow?"

"Some months ago the concern got pinched for money," Doc said slowly, reluctantly. "Had it ceased operating, several thousand men would have been out of jobs. A loan of mine tided them over."

RENNY sank heavily into a chair. At times he felt a positive awe of the mighty bronze man. This was one of the occasions.

It was not the fact that Doc was wealthy enough to take an important hand in a commercial project such as this, that took Renny's breath. It was the uncanny way such things as this turned up—the way the bronze man seemed to have a finger in affairs in every part of the world.

Renny knew Doc possessed fabulous wealth, a golden treasure-trove alongside which the proverbial ransom of a king paled into insignificance. Doc had a fortune great enough to buy and sell some nations.

Renny had seen that treasure. The sight of it had left him dazed for weeks. It lay in the lost Valley of the Vanished, a chasm in the impenetrable mountains of the Central American republic of Hidalgo. This strange place was peopled by a golden-skinned folk, pure-blooded descendants of the ancient Mayan race. They guarded the wealth. And they sent burro trains of it to the outside world as Doc needed it.

There was one string attached to the wealth—Doc was to use it only in projects which would benefit humanity. The

Mayans had insisted upon that. It was to be used for the cause of right.

Their insistence was hardly needed, for it would not have received any other disposition at Doc's hands. Doc's life was dedicated to that same creed—to go here and there, from one end of the world to the other, striving to help those who needed help, punishing those who were malefactors.

This was the thing which motivated Doc's every act.

The same creed bound his five men to Doc. That, and their love of adventure, which was never satisfied.

Chapter 12

TREACHERY

THE search for Monk, Long Tom, and Johnny drew a blank.

"I can assure you we searched every stateroom aboard, and every box and bale of the cargo!" declared slant-eyed First Mate Jong. "There was no sign of three prisoners."

"I don't believe they're aboard!" Captain Hickman added.

Captain Hickman had taken to speaking in a low voice when in the presence of the big bronze man. He was completely in awe of Doc, and his manner showed it.

"I'm still betting they're aboard!" Renny grunted. "Unless—"

He wet his lips. His enormous fists became flinty blocks. It had just occurred to him that Tom Too might have become alarmed and slain the three captives, shoving their bodies overboard.

Renny's fears were dispelled by a plain white card they found under the door of the royal suite the next day. It said:

The straw did not break the back of the camel, you may be glad to learn. But it came very near.

TOM TOO.

"That snake is getting cocky!" Renny gritted. "How could the search have missed our three pals, granting they're aboard?"

"No telling how many of the crew have been bribed," Doc pointed out.

THE *Malay Queen* stopped at Honolulu for a few hours. Doc had gotten instructions to the flashy cockney and the disheveled tropical tramp, otherwise Ham and Mindoro, and they all kept close watch on such persons as went ashore.

No sign of Long Tom, Monk, or Johnny was discovered in the close inspection.

Immediately after the *Malay Queen* put to sea again, Doc Savage instituted a single-handed search for his three captive friends. Due to the great size of the liner, the task was a nearly impossible one.

A hundred of Tom Too's corsairs could conceivably have been aboard without Doc being able to identify one of them. Every Mongol, Jap, Chinaman and half-caste was a potential suspect.

Doc began in the hold. He opened barrels, boxes, and bales of cargo. He examined the fresh-water tanks. The *Malay Queen* was an oil burner, and he scrutinized the fuel tanks Then he began on the D deck cabins and worked up.

It was on D deck, well toward the stern, that his hunt produced first results.

He found a stateroom which had been used, but which was now unoccupied.

The mirror was missing.

On the floor was a small smudge. Analyzing this, Doc learned it was the crayon he used for his invisible writing.

These discoveries told him a story. The prisoners were actually aboard. They had been kept here for a time. Monk had been caught trying to leave a secret message on the mirror The mirror had been removed and thrown overboard. Either Monk or his captors had destroyed the crayon by stamping upon it. Probably that was Monk's work, since Tom Too's men would have wanted the crayon to learn its composition.

Doc continued his prowling. It was an interminable task. The *Malay Queen* had more than four hundred cabins. While Doc searched, Tom Too could easily move the prisoners to a stateroom Doc had already scrutinized.

Doc did not finish the hunting. Tom Too struck at their lives the second night out of Honolulu.

Doc and Renny had been ordering meals sent to their suite to keep Tom Too from getting the idea they were subsisting off rations carried in their baggage. The meals which were brought in to them they chucked overboard. This task usually fell to Renny, while Doc watched for enemies.

Gulls were following the *Malay Queen*. Swooping, the birds snatched anything edible which was tossed overside before the articles reached the water.

The birds bolted portions of the food Renny heaved over the rail.

Two of the feathered scavengers did not fly fifty yards before their wings collapsed and they plummeted into the sea, lifeless.

"Poison!" Renny grunted.

The cook and steward who had come in contact with the meal put in an uncomfortable half hour in front of Doc's probing golden eyes. They convinced the bronze giant they knew nothing of the poison.

Captain Hickman was perturbed when he heard of the attempt. He acted as scared as though his own life had been attempted.

First Mate Jong was also solicitous. "Do you wish me to make a second search of the ship?"

"It would be useless," Doc replied.

Jong stiffened perceptibly. "I hope, sir, you do not distrust the personnel of this craft!"

"Not necessarily."

Doc and Renny redoubled their caution.

The next night they found poisoned needles concealed in their pillows.

A few minutes later, when Doc turned on the water in the bathroom, a villainous, many-legged creature hurtled out of the hot-water faucet.

At this Renny's hair stood on end. He was in the habit of carelessly thrusting his big hands under the faucet when he washed.

"I've seen those things before!" he gulped, pointing at the hideous creature which some one had concealed in the faucet. "It's a species of jungle spider, the bite of which is fatal."

"Tom Too must have gone ashore in Honolulu and loaded up with death-dealing instruments," Doc suggested dryly. "It looks as if we're in for a brisk time."

. Shortly after midnight a bomb tore the royal suite almost completely from the liner. Partitions were reduced to kindling. The beds were demolished, the bed clothing torn to ribbons. Two passengers in near-by accommodations were slightly injured.

Doc's foresight saved him. He and Renny were bunking in with the cockney who showed such bad taste in clothes and manners—Ham.

Renny started to race to the scene of the explosion.

Doc stopped him. "Wait. Let Ham go and see how much damage was done."

Ham was not long on his mission.

"A frightful explosion," he reported. "The sides and roof of the royal suite were blown into the sea."

"Good!" Doc smiled.

"What's good about it?" Renny queried.

"We'll hibernate in here and make it look like we were blown overboard," Doc explained. "In the meantime, Ham and Mindoro will keep their eyes open."

Ham and Mindoro kept their eyes open enough, but it netted them exactly nothing.

The *Malay Queen* neared Mantilla, capital city of the Luzon Union. Arrival time was set for high noon.

Doc quitted Ham's cabin, descended to the lower deck, and approached Mindoro. The wealthy Luzon Union politician was more blowsy-looking than ever in his tropical-tramp disguise.

"How much influence have you with the police chief of Mantilla and the president of the Luzon Union, Doc questioned.

"I made them!" Mindoro said proudly. "They're honest men, and my friends. I believe they would lay down their lives for me to a man."

"Then we will send some radio messages," Doc declared.

"You mean you want the liner searched upon arrival?"

"More than that. I want every person aboard questioned closely, and those who cannot prove they have been engaged in legitimate enterprises for the past few years are to be thrown in jail. Can you swing something that radical?"

"I can. And that should trap Tom Too."

"It'll at least put a crimp in his style," Doc smiled.

They repaired at once to the presence of Captain Hickman. The commander of the *Malay Queen* expressed vast astonishment at sight of Doc.

First Mate Jong, looking up from the binnacle, registered popeyed surprise.

"We wish to use the radio apparatus," Doc explained. "Perhaps you had better come along captain, in case the radio operator should object."

Captain Hickman had suddenly started perspiring. The

mere sight of Doc seemed capable of making him break out in a sweat.

"Of course—of course!" he said jerkily.

First Mate Jong left the bridge at this juncture.

"Just a moment, please!" gulped Captain Hickman. "I must give an order. Then we shall go to the radio room."

Crossing to one of the apprentice seamen always on duty on the bridge, the commander spoke in a low voice. The words continued for fully a minute. Then Captain Hickman hurried back to Doc, apologizing for the delay.

They moved toward the radio cabin. The door of the apparatus room appeared before them.

Renny started violently—for he was suddenly hearing a vague, mellow, trilling sound that ran up and down the musical scale in a weirdly tuneless fashion. It was a melodious, inspiring sound that defied description. And it persisted for only an instant.

Renny knew what it was—Doc's tiny, unconscious sound, which he made in his moments of greatest concentration, or when he had come upon a startling discovery, or as danger threatened.

Instinctively Renny looked around for the trouble. He saw it. Wisps of smoke, yellowish, vile, were crawling out of the wireless-room door.

Doc went ahead, a bronze flash of speed. He veered into the radio room. Two operators manned the instruments at this hour. Both sprawled in puddles of scarlet. They had been stabbed to death.

The wireless sets—both telephone and telegraph—had been expertly wrecked. They were out of commission.

Whoever had done the work was gone.

RENNY flung into the radio room. "Now if this ain't a fine mess!" he rasped hoarsely.

Captain Hickman had not entered.

Doc stepped to the door, looked out.

Captain Hickman's revolver blazed in his face.

Doc moved swiftly, as swiftly as he had ever moved before. Even his incredible speed and agility would not have gotten him in the clear had he tried to jump back. But he did duck enough that the bullet only scuffed through his bronze hair.

Before the treacherous skipper's gun could flame again, Doc was back in the wireless cabin.

Renny had whirled with the shot. "What is it, Doc?"

"It's Captain Hickman!" the giant bronze man said with a

sort of blazing resonance in his voice. "He's on Tom Too's pay roll!"

Renny sprang to the door. The snout of a machine gun bristled from either fist. He shoved one into the corridor and let it drum briefly.

A man shrieked, cursed—his profanity was singing Kwang-tungese.

"That wasn't the captain!" Renny rumbled.

He listened. Speeding feet slippered in the corridor from both directions. They were coming nearer. Shots roared.

"They're closing in on us, Doc!"

Doc picked a glass globule of anæsthetic out of a pocket. But he did not use it. Renny could not hold his breath the three or four minutes necessary for the air to neutralize the stuff.

"Use the guns, Renny. Cut our way out of here!"

Renny sprang to the wall. Beyond lay the deck. He shoved one of the little machine guns out, tightened on the trigger, and waved the muzzle with a circular motion.

The terrific speed of the shots made a deafening moan. The bullets worked on the wall like a monster jig saw. A segment larger than the head of a barrel was cut almost completely out. Renny struck the section with his fist. It flew outward.

Renny and Doc pitched out on deck. Only a few startled passengers were in sight.

Doc sped to the nearest companionway. He reached the deck below in a single prodigious leap. Renny followed, waving the guns wildly for balance as he negotiated with three jumps and a near headlong fall the distance Doc had covered in one spring.

Passengers saw the guns and ran shrieking for cover.

HAM and Mindoro came up the grand staircase, shoulder to shoulder, guns in hand. Ham had his sword cane.

A bullet fired from the upper deck screamed past them. Somewhere in the dining saloon the slug shattered glassware. More lead followed.

"Watch it, Doc!" Ham yelled. "A herd of the devils are coming up from below!"

The words were hardly off his lips when snarling yellow faces topped the grand staircase.

Ham's gun hooted its awful song of death. The faces sank from view, several spraying crimson.

"I'm low on cartridges!" Renny boomed. "Ammunition goes through these guns like sand through a funnel!"

"My baggage is in the hold!" Doc said swiftly. "We'd better get to it! There's two cases of cartridges in the stuff."

They raced forward along a passage, Doc in the lead.

Slant-eyed men suddenly blocked their way. Eight or ten of them! They corked the passage.

Hissing, one man struck at Doc with a short sword. But the blow missed as Doc weaved aside. The force of the swing spun the Oriental. His sword chopped into the passage bulkhead and stuck there.

Doc grasped the swordsman by the neck and one leg. Using the man as a ram, he shot forward like a projectile. Orientals upset, squawling striking. Pistols flamed—nasty little spike-snouted automatics which could drive a bullet a mile.

Then Ham, Renny and Mindoro joined the fray. Their super-firing machine guns made frightful bull-fiddle sawings. Before those terrific blasts of lead, men fell.

It was too much for the corsairs. Those able to do so, fled.

Continuing on, Doc and his men descended a companionway to the forward deck. Doc wrenched open a hatch which gave access to the hold. He descended.

The Orientals caught sight of them. They fired a coughing volley. Slivers jumped out of the deck. Slugs tapped the iron hatch. A bullet hit Ham's sword cane and sent it cartwheeling across the deck.

Ham howled angrily, risked almost certain death to dive over and retrieve his sword cane, then popped down the hatch. By a miracle, he was unscratched.

"You lucky cuss!" Renny told him.

"That's what comes of leading a righteous life!" Ham grinned.

They were in the luggage room of the hold. Trunks and valises were heaped about them. Doc dived into this stuff, hunting his own luggage, which had been put aboard in San Francisco.

At the same time, Doc kept a watch on the hatch.

Grimacing in aversion, Ham ripped off his flashy coat and vest. He had already lost the villainous green hat. He took off the blood-colored shoes and flung them out of the hatch.

"I'll go barefooted before I'll wear them another minute!" he snapped.

Renny snorted mirthfully as, an instant later, the red shoes came flying back down the hatch, hurled by some Oriental.

Chapter 13

WATER ESCAPE

SILENCE now fell. This was broken by singsonged orders. Ham and Renny listened to these with interest. The yellow men seemed to be speaking a half dozen tongues from Hindustani, Mongol dialects, and Mandarin, to Kwangtung-ese and pidgin English.

"There must be riffraff from every country in the Far East up there!" Renny boomed.

"I'm surprised at that," Ham clipped. "Tom Too's men in New York were all Mongols or half-castes with Mongol blood."

Mindoro explained this. "The rumors have it that Tom Too's most trusted men are of Mongol strain. Those were naturally the men he took to New York."

Doc Savage had found his trunks. He wrenched one open. Two cases of the high-powered little cartridges for the compact machine guns toppled out.

Doc grasped the edge of one box. He pulled. The wood tore away under his steel-thewed fingers as though it were so much rotten cork.

Mindoro, who was watching, drew in a gasp of wonder. He was still subject to dumfoundment at the incredible strength in those huge bronze hands of Doc's.

"Keep your eye peeled, Renny!" Doc warned. "They're talking about throwing a hand grenade down that hatch!"

It was Renny's turn to be amazed. How Doc had managed to pick the information out of the unintelligible tumult overhead was beyond him.

Renny strained his eyes upward until they ached.

Sure enough, a hand grenade came sailing down the hatch.

Renny's machine gun blared. The burst of lead caught the grenade, exploded it. Renny was probably one of the most expert machine gunners ever to hold back a trigger. The noisy little weapons of Doc's invention, by no means easy to hold upon a target while operating, were steady as balanced pistols in his big paws.

There was quite a concussion as the grenade detonated. I harmed nobody, although a fragment hit Renny's bullet-proo vest so hard it set him coughing. Doc, Ham, and Mindoro had dived to cover in the baggage.

"We can play that game with them!" Doc said dryly. He opened a second trunk, took out iron grenades the size of turkey eggs, and flirted two up through the hatch.

The twin roars brought a yowling, agonized burst of Oriental yells. The attackers withdrew a short distance and began pouring a steady stream of bullets at the hatch.

This continued some minutes. Then the hatch suddenly flopped shut. Chains rattled. The links were being employed to make the cover fast.

A flashlight appeared in Doc's hand. It lanced the darkness which now saturated the hold. Rapidly he tried all the exits.

"They've locked us in!" he told the others grimly.

MINDORO, lapsing into Spanish in his excitement, babbled expletives. "This is incredible!" he fumbled. "Imagine such a thing as this happening on one of the finest liners plying the Pacific! It feels unnatural!"

"I'll bet it feels natural to the pirates on deck," Renny grunted. "This is the way they work it on the China coast. The devils ship aboard as passengers and in the crew, then take over the craft at a signal."

Comparative calm now settled upon the *Malay Queen*. The engines had not stopped; they continued to throb. They were modern and efficient, those engines. Up on deck they could not be heard. Down here in the hold they were barely audible.

"What are we going to do, Doc?" Ham wanted to know.

"Wait."

"What on? They've got us locked in."

"Which is probably fortunate for us," Doc pointed out. "We can hardly take over the ship, even if we whipped the whole gang. And they're slightly too many for us. We'll wait for—well, anything."

"But what about Monk, Long Tom, and Johnny?"

Fully a minute ticked away before Doc answered.

"We shall have to take the chance that they'll be kept alive as long as I'm living—provided they haven't been eliminated already."

"I don't think they have been killed," Ham said optimistically. "Tom Too is smart. He knows his three prisoners will be the price of his life should he fall into our hands. He won't throw away such a valuable prize."

"My thought, too," Doc admitted.

Mindoro was moved to put a delicate question. Perhaps the strain under which he was laboring made him blunt, for he ordinarily would have couched the query in the most diplomatic phraseology, or not have asked it at all.

"Would you turn Tom Too loose to save your friends?" he quizzed.

Doc's reply came with rapping swiftness.

"I'd turn the devil loose to save those three men!" He was silent the space of a dozen heartbeats, then added: "And you can be sure that when they joined me, they'd turn around and catch the devil again."

The others were silent. Mindoro wished he hadn't asked the question. There was something terrible about the depth of concern the big bronze man felt over the safety of his three friends—a concern which had hardly showed in his manner, but which was apparent here in the darkness of the hold, where they could not see him, but only hear his vibrant voice.

Minutes passed, swiftly at first, then slowly. They dragged into hours.

THE engines finally stopped. A rumble came from forward.

"The anchor dropping!" Doc declared.

"Any idea where we are?" Ham wanted to know.

"We've about had time to reach the harbor of Mantilla."

The four men listened. The great liner whispered with faint sound, noises too vague for Ham, Renny, and Mindoro to identify. But Doc's highly tuned ears, his greater powers of concentration, fathomed the meaning of the murmurings.

"They're lowering the boats."

"But this craft was supposed to tie up at the wharf in Mantilla," said Mindoro.

Silence fell. They continued to strain their eardrums until they crackled protest.

This continued fully half an hour.

"The liner anchored in about seventy feet of water," Doc stated.

"How can you tell?" Ham asked surprised.

"By the approximate number of anchor-chain links that went overboard. If you had listened carefully, you'd have noted each link made a jar as it went through the hawse hole."

Ham grinned. He had not thought of that. He gave their flashlight a fresh wind. This light used no battery, current being supplied by a spring-driven generator within the handle.

"Things have sort of quieted down," murmured Renny, who had been sitting with an ear pressed to a bulkhead.

Mounting the metal ladder to the hold hatch, he struck the lid fiercely with his fist. Bullets instantly rattled against it. A few, driven by rifles, came inside. Renny descended hastily.

"They haven't gone off and left us!" he grunted.

"What d'you reckon they're planning to do?" Ham questioned.

"Nothing pleasant, you may be assured," said Mindoro.

Mindoro's nerve was holding up. He showed none of the hysteria which comes of terror. His voice was not even unduly strained.

Faint sounds could now be heard on the deck immediately above. Wrack their ears as they might, Doc and his men could not tell what was happening.

"They're doing something!" Renny muttered, and that was as near as they came to solving the mystery.

The sounds ceased.

Mindoro's anxiety moved him to speak. "Hadn't we better do something?"

"Let them make the first move," Doc replied. "We're in a position down here to cope with any emergency."

Mindoro had his doubts; it looked to him as if they were merely trapped. But Ham and Renny understood what Doc meant—in Doc's baggage there was probably paraphernalia to meet any hostile gesture the pirates might make.

"This waiting gets in my hair!" Renny thumped. "I wish something would happen! Anything——"

Whur-r-room!

The hull of the liner jumped inward, shoved by a monster sheet of flame and expanding gases.

The Orientals had lowered dynamite overside and exploded it below the water line!

TRUNKS and valises were shoveled to the opposite side of the hold by the blast. Fortunately the liner hull absorbed much of the explosion force.

Doc and his three companions extricated themselves from the mess of baggage.

A wall of water poured through the rent in the hull. It scooted across the hold floor. A moaning, swirling flood, it rose rapidly.

Instinct sent Ham, Renny and Mindoro to the ladder that led to the deck hatch. They mounted.

"We can blow open the hatch with a grenade!" Ham clipped.

"Not so fast!" Doc called from below. "You can bet the pirates will be standing by with machine guns. They'll let you have a flock of lead the minute you show outside!"

A second explosion sounded, jarring the whole liner. This one occurred back near the stern.

"They're sinking the boat!" Mindoro shouted. "We'll be trapped in here!"

In his perturbation, he decided to ignore Doc's warning. He started on up the ladder to the hatch. But Renny flung up a big hand and held him back.

"Doc has got something up his sleeve!" Renny grunted, "so don't worry!"

Down in the hold, water sloshing to his waist, Doc was plucking out the contents of another of his trunks. He turned his flashlight on his three companions, then flung something up to them. He followed it with another—a third.

Renny caught the first, passed it up to Mindoro, and rumbled: "Put it on!"

The objects consisted of helmetlike hoods which fitted over the entire head and snugged with draw strings around the neck. They were equipped with gogglelike windows.

They were compact little diving hoods. Air for breathing was taken care of by artificial lungs carried in small back packs. Respiration was through a flexible hose and a mouthpiece-nose-clip contrivance inside the mask.

There were also lead bracelets fitting around their ankles, and heavy enough to keep their feet down.

Renny assisted Mindoro to don the diving hood, then put one on himself. Ham's sharply cut, hawklike face disappeared in another; he took a fresh grasp on his sword came and waited.

Doc, his bronze head already enveloped in one of the hoods, was delving into other of his trunks, and making bundles of objects which he removed.

The generator-operated flashlights were waterproof. They furnished a pale luminance in the rushing, greasy floor that rapidly filled the hold.

THE liner sank. The boilers aft let go with hollow explosions. Water whirled a maelstrom in the hold, tumbling the four men and the numerous pieces of baggage about.

Water pressure increased as the vessel sought the depths. But at seventy feet it was not dangerous. With a surprisingly gentle jar, the *Malay Queen* settled on the bottom.

Locating each other by the glowing flashlights, the four men got together. Each carried a light.

Doc had four bundles ready—one for each man.

Thanks to the water-tight hoods, it was not necessary to keep the mouthpiece of the air hose between their lips at all times. By jamming their heads together, they could talk.

"Each of you carry one of these bundles," Doc directed. "We'll leave by the hole their dynamite opened—provided the ship is not resting so the sand has closed it."

The hole was open. They clambered through, using care that razor edges of the torn hull did not perforate the waterproof hoods.

The depths were chocolate-colored with mud raised by the sinking *Malay Queen*. The men joined hands to prevent being lost from each other. Doc leading, they churned through soft mud, away from the ill-fated liner. They were forced to lean far over, as though breasting a stiff gale, to make progress.

The water changed from chocolate hue to a straw tint, then to that of grapefruit juice, as the mud became less plentiful. Where the sea was clear, Doc halted the procession. They held conclave, heads rammed tightly together.

"Wait here," Doc directed. "If I'm not back in fifteen minutes, head for shore."

"How can we tell where shore is?" Mindoro demanded.

Doc produced a small, water-tight compass. He handed this to Ham.

"Granting that they sank the liner in Mantilla bay, the town itself will be due east. Head that direction."

Doc now twisted a small valve on the "lung" apparatus of his diving hood. This puffed out the slack lower portion of the hood with air—gave him enough buoyancy to counteract the weight of the lead anklets. He lifted slowly, leaving his three companions behind on the bottom, an anxious group.

Nearing the surface—this was evidenced by the glow of sunlight—Doc adjusted another valve in the hood until his weight equaled that of the water he displaced, so that he neither rose or sank.

He paddled upward cautiously. If his guess was right, the pirates would be standing by in small boats, revolvers and machine guns in hand.

Doc wanted them to know he was alive.

This was of vital importance. As long as Tom Too knew he faced the menace of Doc Savage, he would not be liable to slay Doc's three friends, whom he held prisoner. Or were the three captives still alive?

They were. The instant Doc's head topped the surface, he saw Monk, Long Tom, and Johnny.

Chapter 14

HUNTED MEN

MONK, big and furry, clothes practically torn off, crouched in the bow of a near-by lifeboat. He was shackled with heavy chains and metal bands.

The pale electrical wizard, Long Tom, and the bony, archæologist, Johnny, were seated on a thwart in front of Monk. They were braceleted with ordinary handcuffs.

Other lifeboats and some launches swarmed the vicinity. Yellow men gorged them to the gunwales. Gun barrels bristled over the boats like naked brush.

Every slant eye was fixed on the spot where the *Malay Queen* had gone down. The sea still boiled there. Wreckage drifted in confusion, deck chairs, some lounge furniture, a hatch or two, and lesser objects such as shuffleboard cues and ping-pong balls. A pall of steam from the blown boilers hung above Mantilla Bay.

Doc sank and stroked toward the small craft which held his three friends.

He was hardly under the surface when a terrific explosion occurred in the water near by. It smashed the sea against his body with terrific force.

Swiftly he let all the air out of his diving hood. He scooted into the depths.

He knew what had happened. Some of the corsairs had glimpsed him and hurled a grenade.

Doc swam with grim, machinelike speed. Rifle bullets wouldn't reach him below the surface. But the grenades, detonating like depth bombs, were a grisly menace. He'd have to give up the rescue of his three men. He had no way of getting them ashore.

Chun-n-g!

Then a second grenade loosened. It couldn't have been many feet away. The goggles of Doc's diving hood were crushed inward. Gigantic fists seemed to smash every inch of his bronze frame.

Not missing a stroke in his swimming, Doc shook the glass goggle fragments out of his eyes. No serious damage had been done. He would merely have to keep the mouthpiece-nose-clip contrivance of the "lung" between his lips as long as he was beneath the surface.

His remarkable ability to maintain a sense of direction under all circumstances enabled him to find the three he had left beneath the waters.

Grenades were still exploding beneath the surface. But the blasts were so distant now as to be harmless.

Leaning far over against the water, the four men strode shoreward. Coming to a clear patch of sand, Doc halted, and, with a finger tip, wrote one word.

"Sharks!"

Doc had seen a pilot fish of a shark-following species.

After that warning they kept alert eyes roving the surrounding depths. Fortunately, however, they were not molested.

The bottom slanted upward; the water became translucent with sunlight. They were nearing shore. A roaring commotion passed over their heads, evidently a speed boat.

Upright wooden columns appeared suddenly, thick as a forest, shaggy with barnacles—the piling of a wharf.

Doc led his men into the forest. They rose cautiously to the top.

No one observed them in the shadowy thicket of piling.

Out on the bay, boats scurried everywhere. Some were motor driven, some propelled by stringy yellow oarsmen.

Doc removed his diving hood. The other three followed his example.

"I know a spot ashore where we will be safe," Mindoro declared. "It is one of the rendezvous used by my secret political society."

"Let's go," said Doc.

Shoving themselves from pile to pile, they reached a hawser end which chanced to be dangling. Doc, tugging it, found the upper terminus solid.

He mounted with simian speed and ease. The wharf was piled with hemp bales. Near by yawned a narrow street.

Now the others climbed up. They sprinted for the street—and stopped.

A squad of Mantilla police stood there. They held drawn guns.

"*Bueno!*" exploded Mindoro in Spanish. "We are safe!"

Ham and Renny scowled doubtfully. The police did not look friendly to them. Their doubts were justified an instant later.

"Fire!" shrieked the officer in command of the squad. "Kill the dogs!"

Police pistols flung up—targeted on the vital organs of Doc and his three companions.

Ham, Renny, Mindoro—all three suddenly found themselves scooped up and swept to one side by Doc's bronze right arm.

Simultaneously a small cylinder in Doc's left hand spouted a monster wad of black smoke. The cylinder, of metal, had come from the bundle Doc was carrying. The smoke pall spread with astonishing speed.

Police guns clapped thunderously in the black smudge. Bullets caromed off cobbles, off the building walls. The treacherous officers dashed about, searching savagely. Some had presence of mind to run up and down the street until clear of the umbrageous vapor. They waited there for the bronze giant and his companions to appear.

But they did not put in an appearance.

Not until the smoke was dissipated by a breeze, fully ten minutes later, did the would-be killers find an open door in one of the buildings walling the street. By that time Doc, Ham, Renny and Mindoro were many blocks away.

MINDORO was white with rage. From time to time he shook his fists in expressive Latin fashion.

"That group of police was composed of Tom Too's men!" he hissed wrathfully. "That explains their action. The devil must have enough of his followers, or men whom he has bribed, on the police force to take over the department when he decides to strike."

Doc replied nothing.

Ham and Renny exchanged doubtful glances. It looked as if they had stepped from the frying pan into the fire. Tom Too's plot was tremendous in scope. If the police were under the domination of the buccaneers, Doc would be in for some tough sailing.

They entered thickly crowded streets. The excitement in the bay seemed to be·attracting virtually every inhabitant of Mantilla. Many, curious, were making for the bay at a dead run.

A tight group, Doc and his men breasted this tide of humanity. They avoided such of the Mantilla constabulary as they saw.

Mindoro soon led them into a small shop. The proprietor, a benign-looking Chinese gentleman, smiled widely at Mindoro. They exchanged words in Mandarin.

"To have you back is like seeing the sun rise after a long and dark and horrible night," murmured the Celestial. "This lowly person presumes you wish to use the secret way."

"Right," Mindoro told him.

In a rear room a large brass gong hung. It was shaped like a gigantic cymbal, such as drummers hammer. This was moved aside, a section of the wall behind opened, and Doc and his companions entered a concealed stairway.

This twisted and angled, became a passage even more crooked, and finally turned into another stair flight.

They stepped into a windowless room. The air was perfumed faintly with incense. Tapestries draped the walls; thick rugs matted the floor; comfortably upholstered furniture stood about. There was a cabinet laden with canned and preserved foods. A well-stocked bookcase stood against one wall.

A very modern radio set, equipped for long and short-wave reception, completed the fittings.

"This is one of several hidden retreats established by my secret society," Mindoro explained.

Ham had carried his sword cane throughout the excitement. He used it to punch the soft upholstery of a chair, as if estimating its comfort.

"How did you come to organize your political society in secrecy?" he asked. "That has been puzzling me all along. Did you expect a thing like this Tom Too menace to turn up?"

"Not exactly," replied Mindoro. "Secrecy is the way of the Orient. We do not come out in the open and settle things in a knock-down-and-drag-out fashion, as you Americans do. Of course, the secrecy was incorporated for our protection. The first move in seizing power is naturally to wipe out those who are running things. In the Orient, secret societies are not regarded as the insidious thing you Yanks consider them."

"Our first move is to find how things stand here," Doc put in.

"I shall secure that information," Mindoro declared. "I intend to depart at once."

"Can you move about in safety?"

"In perfect security. I will not go far—only to dispatch messengers to my associates."

Before departing, Mindoro showed Doc and the others three hidden exits from the room for use in emergency.

"These walls are impervious to sound," Mindoro explained. "You can play the radio. We have more than one broadcasting station here in Mantilla."

One of the concealed passages swallowed him.

Doc clicked on the radio. It was powerful. He picked up broadcasts from Australia, from China, from Japan, as he ran down the dial. He stopped on one of the local Mantilla stations. An announcer was speaking in English.

"We interrupt our musical program to read a news bulletin issued by the chief of police concerning the sinking of the liner *Malay Queen* in the Mantilla harbor not many minutes ago," said the radio announcer. "It seems that a group of four desperate criminals were trapped aboard the liner. They resisted arrest. Although many of the liner's passengers joined in the attempt to capture them, the four criminals took refuge in the hold. There they exploded a bomb which sank the vessel."

"Holy cow!" Renny burst forth. "They've explained the whole thing with a slick bunch of lies!"

"This Tom Too is smooth!" clipped Ham, with the grudging admiration of one quick thinker for another. Ham himself was probably as mentally agile a lawyer as ever swayed a jury.

"Due to the foresight of brave Captain Hickman of the *Malay Queen*, the passengers were all taken ashore in safety before the four desperadoes exploded the bomb which sank the liner," continued the voice from the radio. "Several Mongols and half-castes among the passengers, who sought courageously to aid in subduing the four bad men, were slain."

"They're even making Tom Too's gang out as heroes!" Renny groaned.

"Flash!" suddenly exclaimed the radio announcer. "We have just been asked to broadcast a warning that the four killers reached shore from the sinking *Malay Queen!* They are now somewhere in Mantilla. Their names are not known, but their descriptions follow."

Next came an accurate delineation of how Doc, Ham, Renny, and Mindoro looked.

"These men are desperate characters," finished the radio announcer. "The police have orders to shoot them on sight. And Captain Hickman, skipper of the ill-fated *Malay Queen*, is offering a reward of ten thousand dollars for the capture of each of these men, dead or alive, preferably dead."

Music now came from the radio. Doc turned over to the short wave side and soon picked up the station of the Mantilla police. Mantilla seemed to have a very modern police department. The station was repeating descriptions of Doc and the others, with orders that they be shot on sight.

"It looks kinda tough," Renny suggested dryly.

"Tough!" snorted Ham. "It's the dangedest jam we were ever in!"

MINDORO was long-faced with worry when he returned.

"The situation is indeed serious," he informed them. "My associates succeeded in trapping one of Tom Too's Mongols. They scared the fellow into talking. The information they secured was most ominous. Tom Too is ready to seize power!"

"Exactly how is it to be managed!" Doc questioned.

"The physicians who attend the president have been bribed," Mindoro explained. "The president will be poisoned, and the physicians will say he died of heart failure. The moment this news gets out, rioting will start. The rioters will be Tom Too's men, working under his orders.

"Tom Too will step in and take charge of the police, many of whom are his men, or in his service because of bribes. They will put down the rioting with an iron hand—a simple matter since the rioting will be staged deliberately. Tom Too will be touted in newspapers and over the radio as the iron man who took charge in the crisis. He will ride into power on a wave of public good will."

"That is the sort of plan which will work in this day and age!" Ham declared savagely.

"It doesn't sound like pirate methods!" Renny grunted.

"Tom Too is a modern edition of a pirate," Doc pointed out dryly. "If he should sail into port with his warships, as buccaneers did in the old days, he wouldn't get to first base. For one thing, the Luzon Union army and navy would probably whip him. If they didn't, a few dozen foreign warships would arrive, and that would be his finish."

A messenger, a husky patrolman on the Mantilla police force, whom Mindoro trusted, arrived bearing a change of garments for all four of the refugees.

Doc studied the patrolman with interest. The officer's uniform consisted of khaki shorts which terminated above the knees, blouse and tunic of the same hue, and a white sun helmet. The man's brown feet and legs were bare of covering.

"Have Tom Too's men sought to bribe you?" Doc asked.

"All same many time," admitted the officer in beach English. "Me no likee. Me say so."

"They tell you who to see in case you changed your mind?"

"They give me name fella come alongside if I want some Tom Too's dolla'," was the reply.

"They told you who to see if you wanted on Tom Too's pay roll, eh?" Doc murmured.

"Lightee."

Doc's golden eyes roved over his fellows.
"Brothers," he said softly, "I have an idea!"

Chapter 15

RESCUE TRAIL

Some thirty minutes later, a husky Mantilla policeman could be seen leaving the vicinity of the secret room to which Juan Mindoro had led Doc Savage, Ham, and Renny.

The cop twiddled his long billy in indolent fashion, as though he had no cares. Yet he covered ground swiftly until he reached a sector of Mantilla given over almost entirely to Chinese shops and dwellings.

Here, he approached the driver of a small, horse-drawn conveyance known as a *caleso*. The driver was leaning sleepily against his mangy pony. The cop accosted him with an air of furtiveness.

"Alee same come by change of mind."

"No savvy," said the surly *caleso* driver.

"Me likee many pesos," continued the cop patiently. "Tom Too got. Me want. Me get idea come to you chop chop. You fixee."

The *caleso* driver's evil face did not change.

"Seat yourself in my lowly conveyance, oh lord," he said in flowery Mandarin.

The cop hopped into the vehicle with alacrity, crossed his bare brown legs and settled back.

The *caleso* clattered down many streets that would not pass as decent American alleys. These were swarming with people either coming from the excitement at the bay front, or going. The inhabitants of Mantilla were of every conceivable nationality, not a few of them a conglomerate of all the others. Mantilla seemed to be a caldron in which the bloods of all races were intermingled.

Several times, policemen or other individuals cast knowing leers at the big cop riding in the *caleso*. This was evidence the driver of the vehicle had corrupted more than one man. The mere fact that a cop was riding in this *caleso* was an indication he was en route to receive a bribe from Tom Too's paymaster.

The *caleso* halted before an ancient stone building.

"Will you consent to alight, oh mighty one," said the driver in Mandarin. The contempt in his beady, sloping eyes belied his flowery fashion of speech.

The big policeman got out. He was conducted into a filthy room where an old hag sat on the floor, cracking nuts with a hammer and a block of hardwood.

Only a close observer would have recognized the three irregularly spaced taps which the old crone gave a nut as a signal.

A door in the rear opened. The *caleso* driver herded the cop into a passage. The place smelled of rats, incense, and cooking opium.

They reached a low, smoky room. Perhaps a dozen Orientals were present, lounging about lazily.

Three men were manacled in a single pile upon the floor—handcuffed ankle to ankle and wrist to wrist.

They were Monk, Long Tom, and Johnny.

The *caleso* driver shoved the big cop.

"Step inside, oh resplendent one," he directed with a thinly veiled sneer. "Tom Too is not here, but his lieutenants are."

The next instant the *caleso* driver smashed backward to the stone wall. He was unconscious before he struck it.

Some terrible, unseen force had struck his jaw, breaking it and all but wiping it off his face.

THE Orientals in the low room cackled like chickens disturbed on a roost. The cackling became enraged howling.

Over the excited bedlam penetrated a sound more strange than any ever heard in that ill-omened room. A sound that defied description, it seemed to trill from everywhere, like the song of a jungle bird. It was musical, yet confined itself to no tune; it was inspiring, but not awesome.

The sound of Doc!

The human pile that was Monk, Long Tom, and Johnny went through an upheaval.

"Doc!" Monk squawled. "By golly, he's found us!"

The form in the airy garb of a Mantilla cop seemed to grow in size, to expand. A giant literally materialized before the eyes of those in the room—a giant who was Doc Savage.

Doc spat out bits of gum he had used to change the character of his face. He whipped forward, and there was such speed in his motion that he semed but a shadow cast across the gloomy den.

The first Oriental in his path dodged wildly. The fellow apparently got clear—the tips of Doc's sinewy bronze fingers, now stained brown, barely touched the man. Yet the slant-eyed one dropped as though stricken through the heart.

A Mongol plucked a revolver from the waistband of his slack pantaloons. It tangled in the shirt tail which hung outside his trousers. He fought to free it. Then there was a sound like an ax hitting a hollow tree, and he fell.

The heavy hardwood stub of the cop's club had knocked him senseless.

Another man was touched by the tips of Doc's fingers. Then two more. The trio were hardly caressed before they became slack, senseless heaps upon the floor.

"His touch is death!" shrieked a Mongol.

That was exaggerated a little. Doc only wore metal thimbles upon his finger tips, in each of which was a needle containing a drug which put a man to sleep instantly. And kept him asleep for hours!

The thimbles were so cleverly constructed that only a close examination would disclose their presence.

Another Oriental went down before Doc's magic touch.

Gun muzzles began lapping flame. Lead shattered the oil lamp which furnished the only illumination.

Putting out the light was a mistake. With the darkness came terror. Yellow men imagined they felt the caress of those terrible fingers. They ducked madly, struck with fury, and sometimes hit each other. Two or three separate fights raged. Coughing guns continued to add to the bedlam.

Panic grew.

"The outer air is sweet, my brothers!" shrilled a voice in Mandarin.

No other impetus was needed. The Mongols headed for the door like skyrockets. Reaching the street, each vied with the other to be the first around the nearest corner.

The old hag lookout, who had made her nut-cracking a signal, had been bowled over in the rush. But now she legged after them.

MONK, Long Tom, and Johnny were scrambling about in their excitement.

"Hold still, you tramps!" Doc chuckled.

His casehardened bronze hands closed over Johnny's handcuffs. They tightened, strained, wrenched—and the links snapped.

Johnny was not surprised. He had seen Doc do things like this on other occasions. Long Tom's bracelets succumbed to the bronze man's herculean strength.

Monk's irons, however, were a different matter. Monk

himself possessed strength far beyond the usual—sufficient to break ordinary handcuffs. His captors must have discovered that—the time he broke loose to write the message on the mirror—and decorated him with heavier cuffs. The links that joined them were like log chains.

"They moved you to various parts of the liner, so I couldn't find you, didn't they?" Doc asked.

"We were changed to different staterooms half a dozen times," Monk told him. "Doc, I don't see how you lived through that voyage. Practically every man of the crew was on Tom Too's pay roll, to say nothing of the swarm of pirates that were among the passengers."

Doc went to work on the locks of Monk's enormous leg and arm irons. They were not difficult. Within thirty seconds, they fell away, expertly picked.

"This place isn't healthy for us!" he warned. "Tom Too's men will swarm around here in a few minutes."

Searching, they found a back exit.

"This place was a sort of headquarters for Tom Too's organization in Mantilla," said Johnny.

Johnny seemed little the worse for his period of captivity. His glasses, which had the magnifying lens on the left side, were missing, however. That was no hardship, since Johnny had nearly normal sight in his right eye.

The pale electrical wizard, Long Tom, had a black eye and a cut lip as souvenirs.

The furry Monk showed plenty of wear and tear. His clothes now amounted to little more than a loin cloth. His rusty red hide was cut, scratched, bruised; his reddish fur was crusted with dried blood.

"They pulled a slick one when they caught us in New York," Monk rumbled. "One of them came staggering into the skyscraper office with red ink spilled all over him, pretending he'd been stabbed nearly to death. He got us all looking down in the street to see his assailant. Then his pals walked in and covered us with guns."

Persons stared at the four men curiously. Thinking the cop had arrested the other three, some sought to follow. But they were soon outdistanced. Doc hurried the pace.

They returned to Mindoro's hide-out by a circuitous route.

THERE was a hilarious reunion when they all met in the secret, sound-proofed room. Renny cuffed Johnny and Long Tom about delightedly with his huge paws, rumbling, "I'll teach you two guys to go and get yourselves caught and cause us so much trouble!"

Monk leered at his old sparring mate, Ham, rubbed his hairy paws in anticipation, and started forward.

Ham flourished his sword cane menacingly. "I'll pick your teeth with this thing if you lay a hand on me, you ugly missing link!"

Mindoro stood to one side. He was smiling a little, the first time his face had registered anything but gloom for some days past. The fact that this remarkable group of fighting men were together again had heartened him.

"I had a lucky break in hunting them," Doc told Mindoro. "They were being held at the place where I was taken to be put on Tom Too's pay roll. I expected a more difficult hunt."

The big policeman with whom Doc had changed clothes was still present. Doc gave him back his garments.

The boisterous greeting subsided. Doc put questions to the three he had rescued.

"Did you overhear anything concerning Tom Too's plans?" he asked.

It was Johnny, the bony archæologist, who answered. "A little. For instance, we learned how he is going to take over the government of the Luzon Union."

Johnny's information jibed with that obtained by Mindoro, it developed as he talked.

"Tom Too's more villainous and ignorant followers are going to stage the rioting," Johnny continued. "They must be a mighty tough crew, because he hasn't dared to let them come into Mantilla. They're camped on a small island to the north, the whole lot of them, waiting for word which will bring them here."

"He hasn't let them come into Mantilla because he's afraid they'd start looting ahead of time," Long Tom put in. "I don't think he has any too strong a hold over the pirates camped on the island."

"I *know* he hasn't!" interposed Monk. "I heard talk which revealed the pirates on the island are tired of waiting, and are on the point of rebellion. They figure themselves as liable to get shot in the rioting, so they're not so hot about their part in the whole plot. There was talk that they intended to make a raid of their own on Mantilla, in the old-fashioned pirate way."

"They must be ignorant!" Ham snapped. "Otherwise, they'd know a thing like that won't work in this day and age."

"Of course they're dumb," Monk grinned. "Tom Too went up there the minute he landed. He knows he's got to calm them down, or his scheme to seize the Luzon Union is shot."

Mindoro put in a sharp query. "What does Tom Too look like?"

"We didn't see him," Monk said sorrowfully. "We've got no idea what he looks like."

"How did Tom Too go to the island?" Doc asked sharply.

"By boat."

"You sure?"

"I sure am!"

"That's swell."

"Huh?" Monk grunted wonderingly.

"We can get hold of a plane and beat him there," Doc said grimly. "Provided you heard the name of the island?"

"Shark Head Island."

"I can mark the spot on a map!" declared Mindoro eagerly. "The place is an all-night run up the coast by boat."

Chapter 16

THE BUCCANEER MUTINY

THAT night, a ceiling of black cloud hung at ten thousand feet. Under this, darkness lurked, thick and damply foul as the breath of some carnivorous monster.

The hour was early. Lights glowed through the open walls of huts. Here and there a torch flared as some native went about night duties.

A mile high, just below the cloud ceiling, a plane boomed through the night. Exhaust stacks of its two big radial motors lipped blue flame occasionally. The tips of the single far-flung wing and the spidery rudder mechanism bore no distinguishing lights. The craft was an amphibian—the landing wheels cranking up into wells on the hull when it was desired to make a landing in water. In a pinch, the craft could carry sixteen passengers.

It carried only six now—Doc Savage and his five friends.

Mindoro had remained behind in Mantilla. He had been unwilling to be the stay-at-home, at first. But Doc had pointed out it was highly important that Mindoro assembled his loyal forces and prepare to resist Tom Too's coup d'état.

Mindoro's first move would be to throw a dependable guard around the president of the Luzon Union, so there would be no poisoning. The doctors who had been bribed by Tom Too's men to proclaim the poison death a case of heart failure, were to be disposed of. Doc hadn't inquired just what the disposal would be. It probably would not be pleasant.

It had been a simple matter for Mindoro to secure the plane for Doc's use.

Renny was navigating the plane. This was not an easy task, since they could not see the heavens, or the contour of the land below. Renny, thanks to his engineering training, was an expert at this sort of thing.

Doc handled the controls. Doc had studied flying just as intensively as he had worked upon other things. He had many thousands of hours of flying time behind him, and it was evidenced in his uncanny skill with the controls.

"No sign of a radio working on Tom Too's boat," Long Tom reported.

The scrawny-looking electrical wizard had hoped to locate Tom Too by radio compass.

"That's too bad," he added. "If we could find him, we'd make short work of him."

Due to the darkness of the night, there was no hope of sighting the craft bearing the pirate chief to such of his followers as were camped on Shark Head Island.

"We're getting near the place!" Renny warned, after studying a group of course figures he had scribbled.

"Any chance the presence of a plane will make them suspicious?" Ham wanted to know.

"The Mantilla to Hongkong air mail route is not far from here," Doc pointed out. "Probably they're accustomed to hearing planes."

Several minutes passed, the miles dropping behind, two to the minute.

"There we are!" Renny boomed.

SCORES of camp fires had appeared a mile beneath the plane. Distance made them seem small as sparks.

Monk was using binoculars. "That's the layout, all right. I can see some of them."

"Take the controls," Doc directed Renny.

Renny complied. He was an accomplished pilot, as were all of Doc's companions.

"All you fellows understand what you're to do," Doc told them. "Fly on several miles, mounting into the clouds, until you're sure the motor sound has receded from the hearing of those below. Then you are to cut the motors, swing back, and land secretly in the little bay on the north end of the island."

"We got it straight," said Renny. "The pirates are camped on the larger bay at the south end."

"You sure you want us to stay away from them?" Monk grumbled.

"Until you hear from me," Doc replied.

Doc already had a parachute strapped on. As casually as if he were stepping out of the lobby of the New York skyscraper which held his headquarters, he lunged out of the plane. Safely clear, he plucked the ripcord.

With a swish like great wings unfolding, the silken 'chute folds squirted out. The slight shock as it opened completely bothered Doc not at all.

Grasping the shrouds of the 'chute, he pulled them down on one side, skidding the lobe in the direction he wished to take.

Marine charts of the thousands of large and small islands which made up the Luzon Union group had held a detailed map of Shark Head Island. The bit of land was low, swampy, about a mile long and half as wide. Its name came from the reef-studded bay at the lower end. This was shaped something like the snaggle-toothed head of a shark.

Doc landed on the rim of this bay, perhaps three hundred yards from the pirate camp.

The corsairs were making considerable noise. Tom-toms and wheezy wind instruments made a savage medley of sound. It was Chinese in character.

Doc got out of the 'chute harness and bundled it and the silk mushroom under an arm. Searching through the rank jungle growth in the direction of the buccaneer camp, his golden eyes discerned figures gliding about with the jittery motion common to action of the Oriental stage. From time to time, these persons made elaborate cutting motions at each other with swords.

They were entertaining themselves with some sort of a play.

Doc moved out to the sandy portion of the beach. He scooped several gallons of sand into the 'chute and tied it there. Then he entered the water, carrying the parachute and its burden.

Doc's bronze skin was still dyed with the brown stain he had applied when masquerading as the Mantilla policeman. The stain would not wash off.

He swam out into the bay. Where the water was deep, he let the 'chute sink. It would never be found here.

His mighty form cleaved forward with a speed that left a swirling wake. Near the middle of the bay, he headed directly for the grouped camp fires. They were near the shore.

A hundred yards from them, Doc lifted his voice in a shout. His voice had changed so as to be nearly unrecognizable. It was high, squeaky. It was the voice he intended to use in his new character.

"Hey, you fella!" he shrilled. "Me velly much all in! Bling help alongside!"

He got instant attention. The play acting stopped. Yellow men dived for their arms.

Simulating a man near exhaustion, Doc floundered toward the beach.

A villainous horde bristling with weapons, the pirates surged down to meet him.

Doc hauled himself onto the sand. With fierce cries, a score of men pounced upon him. They brandished knives, a crooked-bladed kris or two, swords, pistols, rifles, even very modern submachine guns.

Doc's iron nerve control was never more evident than at that instant. He lay like a man so tired as to be incapable of another movement, although it seemed certain death was upon him.

"Allee same bling you fella big news!" he whined in his piping voice. "Gimme dlink. Me one played-out fella."

They hauled Doc roughly to the fires. They surrounded him, row after row, those in front squatting so the men behind could see. There were Malays, Mongols, Japs, Chinese, white men, blacks—as conglomerate a racial collection as it would be possible to imagine. Turbaned Hindus mingled with them.

One thing they all had in common—lust and butchery, disease and filth, greed and treachery was stamped upon every countenance.

Doc's jaws were pried apart. He was fed a revolting concoction of *kaoliang* cooked with rice. It was a distinct effort to choke the stuff down. A spicy wine followed. Somebody went for more wine. Doc decided it was time to revive.

"Me stalt out in *chug-chug* boat," Doc explained. Strictly, this wasn't a lie. They had ridden out to the anchored seaplane in Mantilla in a motor boat.

"Him boat stop *chug-chug*. Me swim. Get this place by-by. Me plenty much play out."

"Do you speak Mandarin, oh friend who comes in the water?" asked a man in Mandarin.

"I do, oh mighty lord," Doc admitted in the same flamboyant lingo.

"How did you pass the tigers who watch at the mouth of the bay, our brothers who are upon guard?"

"I saw no tigers, illustrious one," said Doc. That was no lie. He hadn't seen the guards.

"The guardian tigers shall have their tails twisted!" roared the pirate. He whirled, snarling orders for some of his followers to hurry and relieve the guards.

"What brings you here?" the corsair asked Doc.

"It is said that man differs from sheep in that man knows when he is to be slaughtered," Doc said in long-winded fashion.

"You are one of Tom Too's sons?"

"I was. But no man wishes to be the son of a dog that would bite off its tail that it might walk upon its rear legs and be like a man."

The buccaneer was perplexed. "What is this talk of slaughtered sheep and dogs who wish to be men, oh puzzling one?"

Doc sat up. He did not lift his voice very much, for he was supposed to be a man suffering from exhaustion, a man who had come a long distance with important news. Nevertheless, his low and powerful tones carried far enough that several hundred slant-eyed and pasty-faced fiends heard his words.

"It is of Tom Too whom I speak, my brothers," he proclaimed. "The man who is your leader has told you that your share of his design upon the Luzon Union is to play the part of looters, that he may be the hero for subduing you.

"The real truth is that you will be shot down like wild ducks upon the hunting preserve of a rich merchant. Are you such fools as to believe many of you will not die? Tom Too will not hesitate to sacrifice you. He considers you rabble. You are the dog tail which he will cut off, and being rid of you, set himself up as a king.

"Are you without sense, that you think he will divide so rich a prize as you would the money box from a looted junk?"

"Such money as Tom Too draws from the Luzon Union must be taken slowly, as a tapeworm sucks nourishment from the stomach of a fat money changer. There will not be great sums at one time. Do you think he will make you rich men, my brothers? If you do, you are but ostriches with your heads in the sand!"

"You have heard this is what Tom Too intends to do?" asked the spokesman of the pirate men, speaking furiously. "Does he intend to slay us while he is making himself a hero?"

"Why do you think I came here?"

"Truly, that puzzles me."

"I do not wish to see hundreds of our brotherhood meet death," Doc replied gravely. "I have warned you."

Doc had been speaking with all the firmness he could put into his powerful voice. This had the desired results. The pirates were virtually convinced Tom Too intended to double-cross them. No doubt they had harbored such suspicions before, as evidenced by the dissention which was bringing Tom Too here to-night.

"Even now, Tom Too comes to speak honeyed words into your ears," Doc added loudly. "If you are but flies, you will flock to the sweetness of his speech. If you are men, you will mount Tom Too's head upon a tall pole in your camp, that the buzzards may look closely at one of their kind."

This was a bold speech. It would either sway the pirates from their leader, or cause them to turn upon Doc.

"We have indeed considered the head on the pole," smirked the leader of the murderous horde, "and the thought finds favor."

Doc knew his propaganda had done its work.

"Tom Too will arrive by boat," he declared. "Then is the time to act—the instant he arrives."

"Wise words, oh brother," was the reply.

Excitement was mounting in the corsair encampment. Doc had spoken throughout in Mandarin, the principal tongue in China, and the one which most of the men understood. But now such of them as did not understand Mandarin, were getting a secondhand version of Doc's speech.

Doc listened, cold lights of humor in his golden eyes. The talk was making Tom Too out as the blackest of villains—which he certainly was.

"WHEN, oh one who brought important news, will Tom Too arrive?" a slant-eyed devil asked.

"Near the hour when the sun smiles over the eastern horizon," was Doc's wordy reply.

It speedily developed that there would be no sleep in the

buccaneer encampment that night. From a score of matting tents and thatched huts came the steely rasp of swords and knives on whetstones.

The variety of weapons possessed by the cutthroats was astounding. Spears that were nothing but sharpened sticks were being prepared by having the points charred into hardness in the fires.

One yellow man with a face half removed by some sword slash in the past was carefully refurbishing a gun consisting of a bamboo tube mounted on a rough stock. This was charged with the crudest kind of black powder and a small fistful of round pebbles, and fired by applying a bit of glowing punk to a touchhole. It was such a gun as had been used by the Chinese thousands of years ago.

Contrasting greatly with these were a dozen or so late-model Maxims which could spew five hundred bullets a minute.

As their rage increased, the pirates snarled at each other like mongrel dogs. One man struck down another with a sword at some slight. The corpse was ignored, as though it were so much discarded meat.

Even Doc was appalled at the bloody savagery of these outcasts of the Orient.

Seven speedy launches were made ready. Doc gathered these were the only fast craft in the pirate flotilla, the other vessels being junks and sampans and a few old schooners and weatherbeaten sloops.

The corsair fleet was anchored in the bay. Due to the darkness, Doc had not yet seen the vessels. They would probably be a sight to remember.

The hours dragged. Doc mingled with the horde of butcherers, adding a judicious word here and there.

If he could get these human scourges to wipe out their leader, the rest would be simple. Mindoro could assemble a force able to deal with them, even should a large proportion of the Luzon Union army and navy be under Tom Too's domination.

Doc wondered briefly about his five men. He had not heard their plane land. That was a good sign. The pirates had been making a good deal of noise, enough to cover the silent arrival of the plane at the tiny bay which the map showed at the other end of Shark Head Island.

Dawn came up like a red fever in the east. It flushed the clouds which still lowered overhead. It set the jungle birds fluttering and whistling and screaming.

The yell of a lookout pealed, couched in pidgin English.

"Tom Too! Him boat come!"

Chapter 17

THE SUNKEN YACHT

THE yellow horde surged for the boats. First arrivals got the seats, to the howling disgust of those behind. There followed a process of natural selection which resulted in the strongest fighters manning the boats. The weaker ones were simply hauled out by the more husky.

Every slant-eyed devil was madly anxious to go along. Tom Too was as famous a pirate as ever scourged the China coast. A hand in his slaying would be something to brag to one's grandchildren about when one was an old man and good for nothing but to sit in the shade of the village market and chew betel nut.

A toothless giant, great brass earrings banging against the corded muscles of his neck, grabbed Doc and sought to pluck him out of the largest and fastest launch. The pirate never was quite positive what then befell him. But he staggered back with both hands over a jaw that felt as though it had tried to chew a fistful of dynamite which exploded in the process.

Doc had no intention of being left behind. He wanted to see that Tom Too didn't talk the corsairs out of their murderous intention.

"Let us proceed, my sons!" shrieked one of the men.

The launches rushed across the bay, keeping in a close group.

Doc now had a chance to observe the remainder of the pirate fleet. The vessels were anchored in the bay by the score. The red flush of dawn painted them with a lurid sinister crimson glow, making them seem craft bathed in blood.

Many were Chinese junks with bluff lines, high poops, and overhanging stems. These were made to appear top-heavy by the high pole masts and big sails with battens running entirely across. The steering rudders, sometimes nothing but a big oar, hung listless in the water.

Many sampans mingled in the fleet, so small as to be little more than skiffs. Some were propelled only with oars, others with sails. All had little matting-roofed cabins in the bows.

The rest of the armada was comprised of sloops and schooners of more prosaic description.

"Tom Too boat, him come in bay *chop-chop!*" sang a man in beach English.

Doc's golden eyes appraised Tom Too's craft.

The vessel was as pretty a thing as ever graced a millionaire's private wharf. It was a fifty-foot, bridge-deck yacht. Its hull shone with the whiteness of scrubbed ivory. The mahogany of the superstructure had a rich sheen. Brasswork glistened.

Several yellow men stood on the glass-enclosed bridge deck.

"We no waste time in talk-talk!" shouted a pirate furiously. "All same finish job damn quick!"

The group of launches spread out in a half moon. They held their fire until within less than two hundred feet of the pretty yacht.

THEN Maxim guns opened with a grisly roar. The weapons shook and smoked, sucked in ammo belt and spewed empty cartridges. A half dozen slant-eyed men clutched each weapon as though it were a mad dog, to keep recoil jar from throwing it off the target.

Automatic pistols popped; rifles spoke with loud smashes. Doc saw the ancient gun with a barrel of bamboo spit its fistful of pebbles at the yacht like a shower of rain.

Glass enclosing the bridge deck of the yacht literally vanished in the lead storm. The cutthroats inside, taken by surprise, were all but fused together in a bloody mass.

"Sinkum boat!" howled a corsair. "Shoot hole in hull!"

The guns were now turned at the yacht water line. The planking splintered, disintegrated. Water poured in. The yacht promptly listed.

Suddenly there was a terrific blast in the yacht entrails. The hull split wide. A bullet had reached explosive, probably dynamite, carried in the little hold.

The cruiser sank with magical speed. A single yellow head appeared, but the swimmer was callously murdered.

"Tom Too gone join his ancestors!" squawled the killers.

Doc Savage would have liked to inquire which of the men in the cruiser cabin had been Tom Too. But he couldn't do that, for he was supposed to have known the pirate king.

The launchers now cruised about in hopes of picking up the body of Tom Too. Many a slant-eyed Jolly Roger expressed a profane desire to possess Tom Too's ears as a souvenir. Bandying ribald jokes as though the whole affair were a lark, the pirates reached an agreement to smoke Tom Too's head and mount it on a pole for all to observe. His body would be skinned, his hide tanned, and each man presented with a piece large enough for a memento. Human fiends, these!

There was much talk as to who had actually killed Tom Too. Many claimed he had not appeared on deck at all, but had remained below like the hiding dog that he was, and had been slain by the explosion.

They didn't find Tom Too's carcass. Disgusted somewhat, they headed for camp to celebrate.

Much strong Chinese wine would be consumed, pots of *kaoliang* cooked with rice prepared, and those who had opium would divide with those who had none. It would be a jamboree to remember.

Doc Savage ducked away from this uproar at the first opportunity. His work here was done. He would join his waiting friends. A quick flight back to Mantilla, and they would assist Mindoro in setting up machinery which would make short shift of the leaderless pirates.

Doc had not progressed fifty yards from camp when snarling, hissing yellow men set upon him.

THE slant-eyed fellows attacked in silence. Pistols were thrust in their belts. Pockets bulged with hand grenades. Yet they used only the crooked kris and short sword.

It was obvious the assailants wanted to finish Doc without attracting notice from the pirate camp.

Doc sprang backward, at the same time scooping up a wrist-thick bamboo pole which chanced to be underfoot. With this, he delivered a whack that bowled over the first swordsman.

Since they wanted no noise, he decided to make some.

"Help!" he piped in his shrill, assumed tone. "Help! Chop-chop!"

Instantly, pirates surged from the camp.

Doc's assailants abandoned their effort at quiet. They plucked out firearms.

Bounding aside, Doc put himself behind the bole of an enormous tree. Bullets jarred into the tree trunk. They did no harm—the attackers could not even see Doc behind the shelter. The tree was a good five feet thick, hiding Doc from view.

The yellow men rushed the tree, came around it from either side.

They stopped and goggled, eyes nearly hanging out.

Their quarry had vanished as though by magic. For two-score feet up the tree trunk, no branches grew. The possibility that their human game had run up the tree, squirrel fashion, was slow occurring to them.

When they did look up, the foliage at the top of the tree had swallowed Doc.

One of the gang hurled a grenade at the approaching pirates. The explosion killed two men. A short, bloody fight followed. No quarter was given or expected. Four minutes later, not one of Doc's attackers remained alive.

Doc slid down the tree.

"These fella tiy kill me," he explained. "Who these fella? How they get this place?"

He spoke in pidgin. The reply was couched in the same slattern tongue.

"These fella belong Tom Too's bodyguald!"

Cold lights came into Doc's strange golden eyes. "How they get this place?"

"We not know."

A short search was pushed in the immediately adjacent jungle, but no skulkers were found. The pirates repaired to their encampment. The preparations for the celebration went forward, although not as boisterously as before. The buccaneers were wondering how the members of Tom Too's personal bodyguard happened to be upon Shark Head Island.

Doc was doing some pondering also. The thoughts which came to him were not pleasant. He had an awful suspicion Tom Too was not dead, after all.

Within the hour, this suspicion crystallized into certainty.

A WEAZENED little yellow man appeared before Doc. No other corsairs were near.

The shriveled fellow extended a bamboo cylinder.

"This belong alongside you," he smirked.

Doc took the bamboo tube. Inside was a rolled sheet of thick, glossy Chinese paper. It bore writing:

The fox is not trapped so easily, bronze man. I had the foresight to come ashore during the night and send my boat into the bay with only the crew aboard, for I did not trust the rabble you have turned against me.

The gods were with me last night, for I came upon a plane in the bay at the north end of the island. Five men loitered near.

And now, bronze man, I have five prisoners instead of the three whom I held for so long.

Your life is the price which will buy theirs. But I do not want you to surrender. You are too dangerous a prisoner.

You will commit suicide, take your own life, in front of the assembled men of the camp. I will have observers present. When they bring me word of your death, your five men will be released.

No doubt you distrust my word. But I assure you it will be kept this once.

TOM TOO.

Doc read this missive through with the cold expressionless of an image of chilled steel.

The shriveled messenger backed away. Doc let him go, apparently not even glancing toward the fellow.

The messenger mingled with the pirates, dodging about in the yellow horde with great frequency. It was apparent he was seeking to lose himself. Several times, he glanced furtively in the direction of the big brown man to whom he had delivered the message tube.

Doc seemed to be paying no attention. Finally, he entered a convenient tent of poles and matting.

The weazened messenger scuttled out of camp. He took to the jungle undergrowth and traveled with extreme caution. Each time he crossed a clearing, he waited on the opposite side a while, watching his back trail. He discerned nothing to alarm.

Nevertheless, the man was being followed. Doc Savage traveled much of the time in the upper lanes of the jungle, employing interlacing branches and creepers for footholds and handgrips. His tremendous strength, his amazing agility, made the treacherous and difficult way seem an easy one.

The shrunken messenger quickened his pace. He had been promised a reward for delivering the bamboo message tube. Tom Too had told him where it would be hidden, in a hollow tree not far ahead.

He reached the tree, thrust an arm into a cavity in the trunk, and brought out a packet. It was several inches square, very weighty.

"Him heavy like velly many pesos inside!" chortled the man.

Greedily, he tore off the wrappings.

There was a red-hot flash, a leviathan of flame that seemed to swallow the man's body. A mushroom of gray-black smoke spouted. Out of this flew segments of the unfortunate one's carcass, as though the fiery leviathan were spitting it out.

The package had contained a bomb.

Tom Too had planned that this man should never lead any

one who followed him to the hiding place of the master
pirate.

Chapter 18

PAYMENT IN SUICIDE

DOC SAVAGE circled the spot where the weazened man had
died. He sought the trail left by the one who had placed the
bomb. His golden eyes missed nothing, for they had been
trained through the years to pick out details such as went
unnoticed to an ordinary observer.

A vine which hung unnaturally, a bush which had been
carefully bent aside and then replaced, but which had a single
leaf wrong side up—these vague signs showed Doc the course
taken by the bomb depositor. The fellow had come and gone
by the same route.

The trail turned out to be a blank. It terminated at the
beach, where a boat had landed the man and taken him
away.

Taking to the trees for greater speed, Doc hurried to the
bay at the north end of the island. The plane was there,
anchored a few yards offshore.

There was no sign of life about, except the jungle birds
which twittered and screamed and fluttered the foliage.

Doc stood by a sluggish stream which emptied into the bay
a few yards from the plane. He decided to try something.

Moving a little more than a rod down the shore, he
suddenly sped into the open, crossed the narrow beach and
shot like an arrow into the bay. He had appeared with
blinding suddenness, and was in the water almost before an
eye could bat.

Hence it was that a watching machine gunner got into
action too late. A stream of bullets turned the water into a
leaping suds where Doc had disappeared.

The gobble of the rapid firer galloped over the bay surface
like satanic mirth. Then the noise stopped.

The gunner ran into the open, the better to see his quarry
upon appearance. The man was stocky, broad, with a head
like a ball of yellow cheese. He stood, gun ready perhaps a
hundred yards from where Doc had entered the water.

Minute after minute, he waited. An evil grin began to
wrinkle his moon of a face. He had killed the bronze devil!

He did not see the foliage part silently behind him. Nor did he hear the mighty form of a man who glided up to his back.

Awful agony suddenly paralyzed the fellow's arms. He dropped his machine gun. He groveled, struggled, kicked. He was flung to the sand. There he continued his fighting. But he might as well have tried to get out from under the Empire State Building.

He could hardly believe his eyes when he saw the giant who held him was the man he thought he had murdered.

Doc had simply swum under water into the sluggish creek, crawled out and crept silently through the rank undergrowth to the attack.

WITHOUT voicing a word, Doc continued to hold his victim helpless for the space of some minutes. Doc knew the psychology of fear. The longer the would-be murderer felt the terrible clutch of those metallic hands, the more terrified he would become. And the more frightened he was, the sooner he would tell Doc some things he wanted to know.

"Where is Tom Too?" Doc demanded. He spoke in his normal voice, couching the words in English.

"Me not know!" whined the captive in pidgin.

Doc carried the man into the jungle, found a small clearing, slammed the fellow on his back. The prisoner tried to scream, thinking he was to be slain.

But Doc merely stared steadily into the man's eyes. The gunner began to squirm. Doc's golden eyes had a weird quality; they seemed to burn into the soul of the captive, to reduce his brain to a beaten and helpless thing.

The man tried to shut his eyes to shut out the terrible power of those golden orbs. Doc held the man's eyelids apart.

Hypnotism was another art Doc had studied extensively. He had drained the resources of America on the subject, had studied under a surgeon in Paris who was so accomplished a hypnotist that he used it instead of an anæsthetic when he operated upon patients. A sojourn in mystic India had been added to Doc's perusal of the art. And he had conducted extensive experiments of his own. His knowledge was wide.

The gunner was not long succumbing. He went into sort of a living sleep.

"Where is Tom Too?" Doc repeated his earlier query.

"Me not know."

"Why don't you?"

"Me left at this place, watch canvas sky wagon. Tom Too no tell place him go."

Doc knew the man was telling the truth. The hypnotic spell was seeing to that.

"What about the five white men who were in the plane?" he demanded.

The reply was three words that froze Doc's great body.

"Him all dead."

For a long minute and a half, Doc neither moved, spoke, or breathed. The prisoner was not lying, not pulling a trick. The news was a ghastly shock.

"How did it happen?" Doc asked, and his voice was a low moan of a whisper that the gunner hardly heard.

"Tom Too, him use poison gas. Five white men, him sit on canvas sky wagon. Gas come. Five white men fall off, sinkee like log."

"Did you see this happen?"

"Too dalk see. Me hear. Men scleam, make big splash."

Doc was done. He dropped a hand into a pocket, brought it out with the needle-containing metal thimbles affixed to the finger tips. He touched the gunner. The fellow promptly slept.

Doc strode into the water and swam toward the plane. A few yards from it, he suddenly put on a terrific burst of speed. His corded arm shot up, grasped a wing strut. He swung aboard not an instant too soon—a great, slate-colored monster reached unsuccessfully for him, tooth-armored jaws gaping.

A shark! Other triangular fins cut the near-by surface.

Doc showed no perturbation over his narrow escape. But he felt slightly sick. No need to hunt for the bodies of his friends on the bottom of the bay, not with these hideous sea scavengers around.

Doc examined the fuel tanks of the plane, found them half full. He gave brief attention to the feed lines, up near the tanks.

The contents of the plane had not been disturbed. Doc got certain articles which he intended to use. They made a bundle a foot through, nearly four feet long.

He reached shore by the simple expedient of lifting the anchor and letting the breeze drift the amphibian to the beach.

Departing from the spot, he noted several birds lying dead in the jungle. The feathered bodies bore no marks. The gas released by Tom Too had undoubtedly killed them.

Doc did not attempt to search the island. It would have taken many hours to do a thorough job.

He headed for the pirate camp. He made speed, but he was careful of the bundle he carried.

The murderous horde were proceeding with their celebration over the death of Tom Too. They did not yet know he was not dead. The festivities consisted exclusively of drinking, gorging with food, smoking opium, to say nothing of frequent fights arising over disputes about whose bullet had actually slain Tom Too.

Doc singled out a husky half-caste who showed in the way he hogged wine and food that he was of a greedy nature. Several times, this fellow filched a jar of the celebration wine and carried it to his matting tent.

Doc was there to meet him when he arrived with one of the jars. In the seclusion of the tent, a lengthy conversation occurred. Once, when the half-caste learned some surprising news, it seemed certain a fight was imminent.

But a large roll of Luzon Union currency changed hands. After that, the half-caste became all smiles and nods of agreement.

The fellow belted on a big sword and went out to join the celebrants.

For upward of an hour, Doc worked furiously in the matting tent.

Stepping outside, he got a barrel of the gasoline used in the launches. This he placed, the bunghole open, near the matting tent.

His powerful voice pealed across the pirate camp.

"I would speak with all you fella!" he said in beach jargon. "All same come alongside plenty quick!"

Yellow men swarmed over, curious to hear what this giant had to say. They were puzzled about something else, too—the big man's voice had changed. It was no longer shrill, piping, but thunderous with latent power.

Doc surveyed the assemblage, standing just in front of the matting tent.

"I have made fools out of you!" he boomed in ordinary English, which most of the corsairs could probably understand. "I came here deliberately to persuade you to turn upon Tom Too!"

He went on, telling exactly what had happened. He informed them Tom Too was still alive. He flung out the note he had received, letting them read it, such as could read.

He carefully neglected any reference to his jaunt to the bay at the north end of the island, or his grisly discoveries there.

"Tom Too is holding my five friends!" he continued. "If I kill myself, he will release them. Therefore, I shall pay that price, so my friends may go free."

A remarkable change had swept the pirate horde. They glowered at Doc, muttering, fingering knives. The fact that the big man had stated he was going to kill himself to save his friends, made no good impression upon them. They were a callous lot.

"I shall now shoot myself!" Doc shouted. "You will all see my act. You can tell Tom Too."

The situation struck some of the corsairs as ridiculous, as indeed it was. The giant who had deceived them was crazy. Did he think Tom Too would release his five friends, once he was dead? Tom Too never kept his word, unless it was to his interest to do so.

Suddenly a husky half-caste sprang forward, waving his sword. It was the same fellow with whom Doc had conversed at length. The man's pants pockets bulged with Doc's money.

"Snake-dog!" he shrieked. "You stand in flont of my tent and befoul it! Fol that, I kill you!"

He rushed forward angrily.

Doc turned and dived into the tent, as though in flight. He seemed to stumble just inside the door, and fall flat.

Fully fifty pirates saw the half-caste's sword strike. The swordsman withdrew a blade that dripped red, and stepped to the tent door.

"My tent is luined!" he howled. "It shall be destloyed with flame!"

Whereupon, he kicked over the gasoline barrel. Fuel sloshed out. The half-caste struck a match and tossed it into the petrol. Flame instantly enveloped the tent.

The half-caste continued to dance around, as though in a great rage.

A close observer might have noticed three Mongols in the pirate crowd who swiftly planted themselves where they could watch all sides of the burning tent.

The flaming matting popped and cracked. Vile yellow smoke poured upward, mingling densely in the boughs of trees which overhung the spot.

The three watching Mongols squatted low, so there would be no chance of any one running away from the blazing tent without being discovered in the act.

The fire raged fully thirty minutes. The tent had been erected upon a foundation of hardwood poles, and these gave off much heat.

LONG before the fire had burned out, the yellow cutthroats gathered in noisy groups to discuss the fact that Tom Too was still alive, and to ponder on what punishment would be theirs for turning against their master.

The three Mongols, however, took no part in this. They never removed the stares of their slant eyes from the conflagration.

When the remains of the tent had become glowing coals, the trio approached. With long poles, they knocked the embers apart.

They showed satisfaction at the sight of gray-white ash which was unmistakably burned bones. One of them raked out a partially consumed piece of bone and pocketed it.

To make certain, they dug into the earth upon which the tent had stood. There was no tunnel.

Throwing down the sticks, the three strode rapidly away. They did not take particular pains not to be seen. But they made sure none of the other pirates followed them.

The beach sand crunched softly under their bare feet. Birds twittered in the jungle. The clouds had cleared away overhead, and the sun was slamming down a hot glare.

"I did not think the bronze man would actually kill himself, oh brothers," said one Mongol thoughtfully, speaking his native tongue. "But there is no doubt but that he did."

"He did not kill himself," another pointed out. "He was speared by the half-caste."

"And very well speared, too," chuckled the third. "And I have in my pocket a burned piece of the bronze man's bones. Tom Too should think highly of that souvenir."

"No doubt he will! Verily, this bronze devil has not been one thorn in our sides—he has been a whole thicket of them."

The three Mongols stepped into a small sampan, shoved off and paddled to the largest of the anchored junks.

The interior of this craft proved to be fitted in lavish fashion, with many tapestries, paintings done on silk and featuring dragons, rugs, and elaborately inlaid furniture.

Near the high stern, they entered a room which contained a modern-looking radio installation. One man threw the switch which started the motor generators, then seated himself at the key.

The other two Mongols stood beside him. Apparently they thought nothing of the incongruity of their surroundings, the commingling of the splendor of ancient China and the shiny copper wires, glistening tubes, and black insulation paneling of the radio transmitter.

The Mongol operator prepared to send.

There was a flash, a loud fizzing of blue flame from the upright instrument board.

The operator leaped up and made an examination. He found a short length of wire. This had short-circuited two important double-pole switches. The man cursed in the Mongol dialect.

"The apparatus is ruined!" he snarled. "It is strange the wire should fall upon the switches! Where did it come from?"

"Where from, indeed?" muttered another. "It is not electrical wire. It looks like a part of a small iron wire cable."

They discussed the mystery profanely for some minutes.

"We cannot send our news to Tom Too by radio," one complained. "We must now go to him in person."

They quitted the pirate junk.

Chapter 19

TOM TOO'S LAIR

THE Mongol trio now took considerably more pains to see that none of the pirates had followed them. Plunging into the jungle, they turned northward. Occasionally they swore softly at noisy tropical birds; the feathered songsters insisted on following them with many shrill outcries.

Midway up the island, on the east shore, was a tiny inlet. It was not over a dozen feet wide and fifty deep. Branches interlaced a mat above it; creepers hung down into the water like drinking serpents.

A sampan was concealed in this. The boat was about thirty feet long, rather wide, and fitted with a mast. The matting sail was down and hanging carelessly over the little cabin in the bows.

The sampan had a modern touch in a powerful outboard motor.

The Mongol trio were about to step aboard when a startling development occurred.

A kris, sixteen inches of crooked, razor-sharp steel, came hissing out of the jungle. It missed one of the Mongols by inches, and embedded in a tree.

"Some dog has followed us!" rasped one man.

Drawing their own knives, as well as a spike-snouted pistol apiece, they charged the spot from which the kris had been thrown. Their stocky bodies crashed noisily in the tangled plant growth. Birds fled with an outburst of noise fit to wake the dead.

The knife thrower could not be found. There was no sign, not even a track.

"We will not waste more time, my sons," said a Mongol.

They entered the sampan. The outboard motor was twisted into life. The sampan went scooting out of the inlet.

The Mongols in their strange craft looked like a trio of innocent fishermen, for the waters of the Luzon Union swarmed with vessels such as this.

The tropical sun slanted down upon the waves with a glittering splendor. Spray tossed from the bows of the flying sampan scintillated like jewel dust. The air was sweet with salt tang. A hideous slate triangle of a shark fin cut across the bows.

Some four or five miles distant was another island, smaller than Shark Head. Tall palms crowned it. Sand of the beach was very white. The whole islet was like a salad of luxurious green set upon a snowy platter. It fascinated the eyes with its beauty. As the sampan swished close, the stench of the overripe vegetation of the island was like the sickening breath of a slaughterhouse.

The sampan curved around the island, made directly for a part of the beach which seemed a solid wall of plant life, hit it—and shot through into a pond of a harbor.

With a belligerent bang or two, the outboard died. Momentum sent the sampan gently aground.

The three Mongols scrambled over the sail piled atop the little bow cabin and leaped ashore.

MORE flowering plants flourished upon this islet than upon Shark Head. Their blooms were a carnival of color. But the place smelled like a swamp; foul, poisonous.

The Mongols gained higher ground. Here stood a house. It was built of hardwood, with the sides of shutterlike panels which could be opened to furnish relief from the heat.

Some half dozen evil-looking men sat in the main room of the house. A strange tension was noticeable in their attitude. They hardly moved a muscle. And when they did stir, it was done slowly and carefully, as if they were afraid of breaking something. They were like men in mortal fear of an impending fate.

The Mongols dashed in upon this solemn assemblage with loudly boisterous cries of elation.

"Where is Tom Too, oh brothers?" they demanded. "We have news for the master. Great news!"

In their excitement, the trio failed to note the air of terror about those in the room.

"Tom Too is not here," said one of the frightened men shrilly.

"Where did he go?"

"He did not say. He merely go."

The three Mongols could not hold back their news.

"The bronze devil is dead," one chortled. "The man did not have great wisdom, as we had thought. He was a fool. He thought he was saving his five friends. He did not know that the five were dead from the gas we released. So he got up before the dogs who would turn against Tom Too and made a speech, telling them who he was, and saying he was going to shoot himself. But one of the dogs cut off his head with a sword and burned his body in a tent. We watched flames consume the body. And I carry in my pocket a bit of the bronze man's bones, which was not consumed. Tom Too will want that souvenir. Where is the master?"

"He go away!" insisted one of the listeners shrilly.

The three Mongols suddenly perceived the tension in the room. They were surprised.

"What is wrong with you, oh trembling ones?"

The reply to that came from a totally unexpected source.

"They're afraid of gettin' pasted with lead!" boomed a slangy Yank voice.

A curtain across the end of the room suddenly snapped down. Five men lounged there. Each held a terrible little implement of death, a compact machine gun that looked like an overgrown automatic.

The five were Doc's friends—Monk, Renny, Long Tom, Ham, and Johnny.

THE three Mongols had been reared amid violence and death. They knew these five men, knew them for mortal enemies of their kind. They tried to make a fight of it.

Yellow hands sped for knives and pistols.

The half dozen others, who had been sitting so fearfully because they were covered by the guns of Doc's men, decided to aid the Mongols. They had been disarmed, but they dived for anything handy. Three got chairs. Two tore legs off a rickety table. Another seized a wine bottle, broke it, and rushed with the jagged end held like a dagger.

The room went into pandemonium. Knives flashed. Fists swung. Shillelahs whacked at heads. Guns bawled thunder.

The five white men concentrated on the three armed Mongols. Two dropped before the bull-fiddle roars of the frightsome little machine guns. Monk closed with the third. A slap of his hairy hand sent the gun flying from the man's hand.

The Mongol struck with his knife. Monk evaded the blade with an ease astounding for one of his bulk, then pasted the yellow man with a hirsute fist. So terrific was the blow that the Mongol dropped his knife and staggered like a drunk, then fell.

Ham closed with a slant-eyed man who wielded a table leg. He fenced briskly, warding off terrific blows with deft parries of his bared sword cane. An instant later the yellow man sprang back, the ligaments in his wrist severed. Squawling for mercy, he shrank into a corner.

Renny pulped a nose with one of his monster fists. Long Tom and Johnny closed with respective opponents. They did not use their guns again. Bare-handed, they were more than a match for the pirates.

The fray ended as suddenly as it had started. The corsairs lost their nerve, shoved their arms in the air, and joined Ham's victim in screeching for quarter.

"A fine gang of yallerhammers!" Monk complained. "Can't even fight enough to get a man warmed up!"

He picked up the Mongol he had struck. The fellow was the only one of the three messengers now alive.

"So you thought the gas got us, eh?" Monk growled. "Well, it didn't! You turned the stuff loose in the jungle so the wind would blow it toward us. We heard birds dropping dead. That warned us. So we dived overboard. It was dark enough so that we didn't have no trouble gettin' away! Then we hung around listenin' to you guys talk."

The Mongol only rolled his slitty eyes.

"We heard enough talk to learn Tom Too was gonna hole up here!" Monk continued fiercely. "So we made a raft out of two logs and paddled over. We been holdin' your pals here, hopin' Tom Too would turn up."

Ham swung over, sword cane poised ominously.

"This is the bird who bragged he was carrying a piece of Doc's burned skeleton!" he said grimly. "Let's see it!"

Monk searched the prisoner and soon brought the charred bit of bone to light.

Johnny, the gaunt archæologist, took one look at it—and laughed loudly as he turned the bone in his hand.

"That's a hunk of ordinary soup bone—off the leg of a cow!"

Knowing bones was part of Johnny's business. He could look at a skeleton from a prehistoric ruin and tell some remarkable things about the ancient to whom it originally belonged.

"Then Doc ain't dead, after all!" Monk grinned.

"That's fair guesswork," said Doc Savage from the doorway.

A ROAR of pleasure greeted Doc's appearance.

"How'd you work it?" Monk wanted to know.

"Used the old magician's stunt with mirrors to make it seem that I had been stabbed," Doc told him. "One of the pirates was in on the trick and swung the sword. I paid him plenty. The sword blade ran through a wad of cloth soaked with red ink instead of my body."

"Hey!" Monk interrupted. "How'd you get out of the tent?"

"The tent was set on fire. I had sprinkled chemicals on it so there would be a great deal of smoke. Overhead was a large tree branch. I had previously rigged a silk cord, small enough not to be noticeable, over the limb so a stout wire could be drawn up. I climbed that, concealed by the smoke, taking my mirrors along. It was not hard to get to other trees and away."

Doc nodded at the survivor of the Mongol trio. "This chap and his two companions went to a junk and prepared to communicate with Tom Too by radio. I broke off a bit of the wire cable with which I had climbed the tree limb, tossed it onto a couple of switches without being noticed, and put the apparatus out of commission. I figured they'd go to Tom Too in person.

"It was necessary to throw a knife at them to decoy them away from their sampan long enough for me to get aboard and find a place to hide under the sail."

Doc fell silent and let his eyes rove over the room. It was not often that he went into such detail in describing his methods. But finding his five friends alive had made him a bit talkative.

Long Tom whipped aside the curtain behind which he and the others had been concealed for a time. This disclosed an army type portable radio transmitter and receiver.

"This is undoubtedly the set the Mongols intended to communicate with from the junk," he declared. "But where's Tom Too?"

"Did he have a chance to dodge you?" Doc asked.

Ham tapped his sword cane thoughtfully. "He might have. We met two of the pirates on the bay shore, had a little fight, and the others came to see what it was about. Tom Too might have remained behind, seen we had cleaned up on his gang, then skipped out."

"He hasn't had a chance to leave the island!" Monk grunted. "We searched the shore line. There wasn't a boat around. And one man couldn't navigate by himself the log raft we came over on."

Countless times Doc's ability to observe any movement about him, however slight, had proved invaluable. It served again now.

His mighty form whipped aside and down, flaky golden eyes fixed on the door.

Lead shrieked through the space he had vacated. A pistol, firing from the jungle, made stuttering clamor.

"Tom Too!" Renny boomed.

Chapter 20

THE TIGHTENING NET

THE shot echoes were still bumping around over the island when Doc's five men turned loose with the little machine guns. The weapons poured bullet streams that were like rods of living metal. The slugs razored off leaves, twigs, branches the thickness of Monk's furry wrist.

After one volley they ceased firing.

Loud crashings reached their ears over the caterwauling of disturbed birds.

"He's beating it!" Renny shouted.

Doc and his men dived out of the room, leaving the cowering prisoners to their own devices. They weren't important game, anyway.

"Did you get a look at Tom Too's face, Doc?" Ham demanded.

"No. Only his gun shoving out through the leaves. I didn't even get the color of his skin. He was wearing gloves."

They spread out in a line, in the order of their running ability. Doc was far in the lead. Next was Johnny, gaunt and bony, but a first-class foot racer. Monk and Renny, the two giants, trod Johnny's heels. Ham and Long Tom were last, pretty evenly matched, with Ham the hindermost because he was trying to keep thorns from tearing his clothes. Ham was always jealous of his appearance.

"He's heading for the sampan!" Doc called.

An instant later they heard the outboard motor on the sampan start.

Doc reached the pondlike bay just in time to glimpse the stern of the sampan vanishing beyond the curtain of vines which screened the tiny harbor from the sea.

His men came up. They drove a few rasping volleys of lead at the drapery of creepers. Then they ran around the bay. This consumed much precious time.

The sampan was nearly three hundred yards distant, traveling like a scared duck.

If they had hoped to glimpse Tom Too's features, they were disappointed. The pirate leader was not in sight.

"Lying in the bottom of the boat to be out of the way of bullets!" Renny said grimly, and took a careful bead on the distant sampan.

His gun moaned deafeningly. The others joined him. Their bullets tore splinters off the sampan stern and scraped the sea all about the craft. But the range was long, even for a rifle, and they did not stop the fleeing boat.

"Where is the raft you fellows came over on?" Doc demanded.

"Up the beach!" rapped Ham, and led the way.

The furry Monk lumbered alongside Ham. They came to a spot where mud was underfoot, slimy and malodorous. In the middle of this Ham suddenly fell headlong. He floundered, then bounced up, smeared with the smelly goo from head to foot. He waved his sword cane wrathfully.

"You tripped me, you hairy missing link!" he howled at Monk.

"Bugs to you!" leered Monk. "Can I help it if you fall over your own feet?"

However, Monk was careful to keep out of Ham's reach for the next few minutes.

Nobody had seen Monk do the tripping, but there was no doubt about his guilt. He had done worse things to Ham. And it was also certain that Ham would return the favor with interest. The going seldom got so hot that these two forgot to carry on their good-natured feud.

They reached the raft.

"It's a wonder the sharks didn't get you birds, riding that thing," said Doc, surveying the raft.

Monk snorted. He was in high good humor, now that he was one up on Ham.

"This shyster lawyer here wanted to feed me to 'em, claimin' they'd die of indigestion from eatin' me," he chuckled with a sidelong look at Ham. "Fallin' in the mud serves him right for makin' cracks like that."

Ham only scowled through the mud on his face.

The raft consisted of a pair of long logs, crumbling with rot, secured in catamaran form with crosspieces and flexible vines.

Doc eyed the sticks which had served as oars. They were highly inefficient.

"Put it in the water!" he directed. Then he vanished into the jungle.

The raft was hardly in the sea before Doc came back. He was carrying an armload of planks ripped from the house. These were much more suitable as paddles.

"What about the prisoners we left in the shack?" Renny demanded.

"They were still there." Doc exhibited one of the finger-tip thimbles containing the drug-laden needles—thimbles which produced long-lasting unconsciousness. "They'll be there quite a while, too."

They shoved off, taking positions on the shaky raft like a trained rowing crew. In a moment the paddles were dipping with machinelike regularity, shoving the crude craft forward at a fair clip.

Their eyes now sought the sampan bearing Tom Too.

Doc had expected Tom Too to head for the pirate encampment on the south end of the island. But the sampan was skipping for the northern extremity, where the plane lay.

"We're in luck!" Doc said softly. "Tom Too doesn't know the temper of his cutthroats. He could dominate them easily and send the whole horde out to finish us. But he's afraid to go near them."

"Yeah, but he's headin' for our plane!" Monk grunted. "And there's bombs aboard it."

"Oh, no, there's not!" Ham clipped. "I stayed behind a little while last night after we heard the birds falling off their roosts and knew there was a gas cloud coming, long enough to chuck the bombs overboard."

The sampan swerved around the north end of Shark Head Island, entered the little bay, and was lost to sight.

Johnny spat a couple of words that would have shocked the natural science class he used to teach, and chopped at a cruising shark with his paddle. After that every one was careful that his feet did not drag in the water.

"Will they jump out of the water and grab a man?" Monk asked doubtfully.

"Probably not," said Johnny.

They kept their eyes on the little bay at the north end of Shark Head Island. The rattle of the outboard motor, made wispy by distance, had stopped.

Suddenly a shower of what looked like sparks shot into the air around the bay. The sparks were gaudily colored tropical birds. A moment later the froggy moan of plane motors wafted over the sea. It was their starting which had flushed up the birds.

"Why didn't you think to take something off the motors so they wouldn't run, wiseheimer?" Monk asked Ham.

Ham glared through his mud, said nothing. He did not dare dip up water to wash his face, due to the sharks.

Soon the plane skidded up into the sunlight. It wobbled, pitched, in the bumpy air. It flew like a duck carrying a load of buckshot.

"He's a rotten flyer!" Johnny declared.

"A *kiwi!*" Monk agreed.

The plane headed directly for the laboring raft.

Monk reached up and clawed his hair down over his eyes to keep the sun out. "I don't like this! That bird is going to crawl up. He may be the world's worst flyer, but I don't like it!"

RENNY followed Monk's example in getting his hair down on his forehead to shade his eyes from the sun. It was the next best thing to colored goggles. They'd have to look up to fight the plane. And gazing into the tropical sky was like looking into a white-hot bowl.

"We left machine guns on the plane!" he muttered. "It's gonna be tough on us?"

Johnny poked another shark in its blunt, tooth-pegged snout.

Doc Savage seemed unworried. He sat well forward, driving his paddle with a force that made the stout wood grunt and bend. So that his mighty strokes would not throw the raft off course, he distributed them on either side with scarcely an interruption in their machinelike precision.

Renny shucked out his pistollike machine gun and rapped a fresh cartridge clip in place.

"You won't need it," Doc told him.

"No?" Renny was surprised.

"Watch the plane!"

The amphibian came howling toward them. Tom Too was not trying for altitude; he wanted to be low enough to use his machine gun with effect—for no doubt he had found the rapid firers in the plane. His altitude was no more than five hundred feet.

"It's about time it happened!" Doc said grimly.

Doc's prediction was accurate.

Both motors of the amphibian suddenly stopped.

Tom Too acted swiftly. He kicked the plane around and headed it back for Shark Head Island. His banking about was sloppy; the ship side-slipped as though the air were greased.

"He can just fly, and that's all!" Monk grinned. "What stopped the motors, Doc?"

"I plugged the fuel lines close to the tanks," Doc replied. "The carburetor and fuel pipes held enough gas to take the craft upstairs, but no more."

The big bronze man neglected to add that it would have been simpler to cut off the fuel at the carburetors, but that this would not have left enough gas available to get the plane off should circumstances have sent them to the craft in such a hurry that they would not have had time to unplug the fuel lines.

Tom Too was gliding the dead-motored plane at a very flat angle, getting the maximum distance out of his altitude. Probably this was by accident rather than flying ability.

"Holy cow!" groaned Renny. "Is he gonna get back to Shark Head?"

"He will come down about a hundred yards offshore," said Doc after a glance of expert appraisal.

The estimate was close. With a sudsy splash, the amphibian plunked into the sea. It pushed ahead for a time under its own weight. It stopped a bit less than three hundred feet offshore.

Then the ship began to move backward—blown by the offshore breeze.

"He'll be blown right into our hands!" Ham ejaculated.

"Or he'll find the plugged fuel lines!" Monk pointed out.

Tom Too wasted no time hunting for what had silenced the motors, however. Probably he was no mechanic. He appeared atop the amphibian cabin.

He was too distant for much to be told about his appearance. Even Doc's sharp vision could not dintinguish the fellow's features.

One thing they did note—Tom Too carried a large brief case.

The pirate leader reached up and struck savagely at the plane wing. There was a knife in his fist.

"Hey!" squawled Monk. "He's lettin' the gas out of the tanks!"

It was worse than that. Tom Too backed up, struck a match, and flung the flame into the petrol drooling from the punctured tanks.

Flame gushed. It wrapped the amphibian until the craft was like a toy done in red tissue paper. Yellow smoke tossed away downwind, convulsing and boiling in the breeze.

Tom Too sprang into the sea. He swam madly for the shore of Shark Head Island.

Johnny gazed at the sharks cruising about the makeshift raft, then at the distant splashes that marked Tom Too's progress.

"That guy has got nerve!" grunted Johnny.

"Fooey!" said Monk. "A rat will fight a lion if he's cornered."

Doc Savage was standing up, still paddling, the better to watch Tom Too's progress.

Renny also watched. His eyes were second in sharpness to Doc's.

"There goes a shark for him!" Renny bawled suddenly.

They all saw the triangle of lead-hued shark fin cutting toward Tom Too.

"There ain't nothin' I like less than sharks!" Monk chuckled. "But I'm gonna find it hard to begrudge that one his meal!"

Tom Too had seen his danger. He swam desperately. But he did not lose his head. He kept his eyes on the approaching fin. It disappeared.

Tom Too promptly stopped. Doc caught the faint glitter of a knife in the pirate king's hand.

"He's going to handle the shark native fashion!" Renny grunted.

Distance hampered their view of what happened next. But they knew enough shark lore to guess. Sharks do not have to turn over to bite an object in the depths, but commonly do so to seize a man swimming on the surface. The pale bellies offer a warning flash.

Tom Too disappeared from sight momentarily. There was

a splashing turmoil in the water. Tom Too's knife struck repeatedly.

The pirate leader appeared. He swam for shore with renewed energy.

"He got the shark—dag-gone it!" Monk wailed.

Tom Too reached the beach without further incident. He sprinted for the jungle.

Doc's sharp eyes noted something the others missed—Tom Too no longer carried his brief case. Evidently he had dropped it in his short fight with the shark.

The plane was burning briskly. Flame ate into the fuselage. A Fourth of July uproar came as heat exploded machine-gun bullets in the craft.

The ship sank suddenly.

Tom Too vanished into the jungle.

Doc and his men continued to bend their paddles.

They reached the spot where the plane had gone down. A score of yards beyond, the shark Tom Too had slain floated near the surface. The water lashed in turmoil about the carcass—half a dozen other sharks were devouring it.

"Whoa!" said Doc.

Monk wore in his belt a knife he had picked up somewhere. It was a serpentine-bladed kris.

Doc grasped the knife, clipped the blade between his strong teeth, and dropped off the shaky raft. He disappeared in the depths.

"Jimmy!" Monk gulped. "With all these sharks around, Daniel in the lions' den was a piker!"

They waited anxiously. Bubbles gurgled up from the sunken plane. A minute passed. Sixty feet away, cannibal sharks fought with horrible splashings. Another minute groped into eternity.

Doc did not appear.

On the shore, coarse-voiced tropical birds cried like hideous harpies.

Three clapping shots interrupted the birds. Monk ducked as a bullet made cold air kiss his furry neck, nearly lost his balance on the ramshackle raft, but recovered himself.

Tom Too had fired at them—water does not wet the powder in modern pistol cartridges.

Doc's five men sprayed lead at the jungle. There was nothing to show they hit Tom Too. But they kept him from shooting again.

Renny glanced at a waterproof wrist watch. He nearly screamed.

Doc had been beneath the surface a full four minutes!

Ten seconds later Doc's bronze head split the water beside the raft. Doc's bronze hair and metallic skin had a strange quality; it seemed to shed water like the back of a duck; he could immerse himself, and his skin and hair would not seem wet when he reappeared.

Doc's shirt front bulged more than his chest should have made it.

Doc's five men wiped cold sweat off their foreheads. The fact that Doc had remained under water so long was not in itself alarming. They had seen the giant bronze man stay below for incredible intervals. But the sharks made these waters reek death.

"Have any trouble?" Monk asked.

Doc shrugged. "Not much."

At this point a second shark carcass appeared beside the first. The hideous creature had been slain with a single expert knife rip. Monk and the others recognized Doc's handiwork. He had battled the monster under water and dismissed it as "not much."

"Huh!" ejaculated Monk. "What were you doin' way over there? The sunken plane is under us."

"Tom Too had a brief case with him, but dropped it when the shark tackled him," Doc replied. "I dived for it from here, not wanting him to know I was after it."

"You get it?"

The bulge in Doc's shirt front gave answer.

THEY now paddled the raft to shore. Tom Too did not fire at them again—a wise move on his part.

"Make for the sampan!" Doc directed.

They sped northward along the beach.

Monk glanced over his shoulder. "Hey—lookit!"

Wheeling, the rest saw Tom Too. The master pirate had come out on the beach half a mile to the south. He was running for dear life, headed for the encampment of his yellow cutthroat horde.

"I'm in favor of going after him!" Renny boomed. Apparently it did not occur to him that they might not be able to whip several hundred slant-eyed pirates who had been fighters all their lives.

"The sampan!" Doc said impatiently. "We'd better get it and clear out of here."

They resumed their sprint for the sampan, smashing their way through the jungle growth in a short cut across a little headland and reached the beach in short order.

"Good!" rapped Ham, catching sight of the sampan where Tom Too had beached it. "I was afraid he might have jabbed a hole in the bottom, or something."

Renny pointed at the outboard motor.

"Look!" he roared. "The gasoline has been let out!"

The valve of the fuel tank was located in such a position as to spill the emptying fuel upon the sand, where it was hopelessly lost.

"This puts us in a swell mess!" Monk groaned.

Four hardwood paddles reposed on the sampan floorboards. Doc indicated them. "Grab 'em!"

"We can't escape by paddling," Monk pointed out. "The pirates have speed boats. Tom Too will send them after us."

With a mighty shove, Doc sent the sampan into the water.

"We'll get back to the other island!" he declared.

There was no more argument. The sampan surged away from the beach, propelled by lusty paddle strokes.

Ham, between sweeps of his paddle, nodded at the bulging front of Doc's shirt, which held the contents of Tom Too's brief case.

"Do you suppose there's anything worth while in there?" he asked.

"We'll let that slip for a while, and examine it later," Doc said, then leveled an arm. "Tom Too didn't lose much time!"

They all followed Doc's gesture. Around the other end of the island, a pair of junks appeared, together with several speed boats. More craft followed—junks, sampans, launches, and other boats.

The hardwood paddles bent and creaked as Doc's men increased their pace. Water split away from the sampan bows with a steady, sobbing noise. They were making good speed for the palm-crowned smaller island.

"We'll beat them to the island!" Ham decided aloud.

"Yeah—and then what?" snorted Monk.

Doc's five men exchanged bleak looks. They were perfectly aware they had never faced greater odds. They were experienced fighting men, and they knew a fight against these hundreds of pirates could be nothing but hopeless.

A corsair machine gun dropped a shower of slugs some hundreds of yards short. The spent bullets continued to drop in the water, coming closer and closer. But the little island was now but a few fathoms distant away from the men.

The rasp of the sampan keel on the beach was a welcome sound.

Chapter 21

SEA CHASE

Doc and his men piled out. A few rifle slugs made chopping noises in the tangled jungle growth. Doc eyed the belts and bulging pockets of his men.

"Got plenty of ammunition?" he questioned.

Monk grinned wryly. "Not as much as I'd like to have. We've got a couple or three hundred rounds apiece. That was about all we could swim with when we left the plane last night."

"Latch the guns into single-shot fire," Doc directed.

Each man flipped a small lever on his compact little machine gun. The weapons now discharged only a single bullet for each pull of the trigger.

Using a sampan paddle as a spade, Doc set to work digging a shallow rifle pit. He located it slightly within the jungle, so he could quit it without being observed.

The others followed his example, saying no word.

Straight toward the beach plunged the pirate boats. The launches, being more speedy, were far in the lead. The pirates had erected small shields of sheet steel in the craft—their usual precaution, no doubt, when going into battle.

Prows scooping foam, they approached to within two hundred yards. Then a hundred! Their speed did not slacken. A machine gun in the bow of one began to cough bullets through a slit in a metal shield. The lead hissed and screamed and tore in the jungle about Doc and his men.

"Let the first one land!" Doc commanded.

An instant later the leading speed boat hit the beach. It was traveling fast enough to skid high and dry out of the water. The slant-eyed killers, braced for the impact though they were, nevertheless slammed against thwarts and bulkheads.

"Now!" Doc clipped. "Get 'em in the legs and arms!"

His gun spat. The weapons of his men rapped a multiplied echo. They were crack marksmen, these men. They took their time and planted bullets accurately.

Two yellow men fell out of the launch almost together, hit in the legs. Pain made them squall noisily. Others cackled in agony as slugs, placed with uncanny precision, took them in the hands and arms.

There was psychology behind Doc's command not to kill. One wounded Oriental, yelling bloody murder, could do more to spread fear among his fellows than three or four killed instantly.

Bedlam seized the launch occupants. They could not even see Doc and his men. A tight group, they sought to charge. Those in the lead went down, legs drilled.

Howling, the gang ran back and tried to shove the launch into the water. They were not sufficient in number for the job. In remorseless succession, these also fell.

"Now—the other launches!" Doc ordered.

The volley he and his men fired sounded ragged, scattered. But hardly a bullet went wild.

The nearer launches, four in number, could not hold up before shooting like this. One careened about madly, the helmsman pawing a drilled shoulder, and barely missed crashing another craft. Then all four sheered off, the occupants expressing their opinion of Doc and his men in assorted tongues.

They were going to await the arrival of the heavier junks and sampans.

Monk, flattened in the pit he had scooped, asked Doc: "What now?"

Doc's pit was in the jungle to the right. No answer came from the spot. Puzzled, Monk squirmed up to look.

Doc was gone. He had vanished silently the instant the fight was over.

No more than a minute passed before Doc returned. He bore a bulky object—the army-type portable radio transmitter and receiver which Tom Too had left in the island cabin.

Doc gave a short gesture of command. The men plunged out of the jungle and leaped for the speed boat stranded on the beach.

A wounded pirate shot at them, but he was wounded in the arm, and missed. Doc fired a single bullet, and the corsair shrieked as the lead mangled his hand. The other yellow men fled, dragging themselves along or running furiously, depending on where they were hit.

Doc and his five aids laid hands on the launch, strained, and ran it back into the surf.

Out to sea, the pirates suddenly saw the purpose of Doc's strategy in permitting the most speedy craft to land. He was seizing the fast little vessel!

The slant-eyed buccaneers headed for the island again.

Machine guns cackled from their boats, rifles whacked spitefully.

Doc shoved the nose of their own launch around while his men sprang aboard. Renny worked over the motor. The propellers had not been damaged by the forcible beaching.

Lead clanged on the sheet-steel shield, chewed splinters off the gunwales, and, hitting in the water near by, dashed spray over them.

Doc and the others returned the fire with slow precision while Renny fought the motor. The engine caught with a blubbery roar. The light hull surged forward, the propellers flinging water up behind the stern.

At the tiller, Doc sent the boat parallel to the beach. In a moment they were stern-on to their enemies, rendering the steel bullet shield useless.

Doc wrenched the shield from its mounting. "Put it up in the stern."

Monk did that job. He howled wrathfully as lead hit the metal plate, transferring a sting to his hands. Renny lunged to help him, then grunted loudly and clapped a hand to the upper part of his left arm. He had been hit. He tore off the sleeve of his shirt with a single wrench.

"Missed the bone an inch!" he decided.

"We're going to make it!" Ham yelled. He was using the tip of his sword cane to jam a wadded handkerchief into a bullet hole in the launch hull near the water line.

Doc put the rudder hard over. The launch veered to the right—and was suddenly sheltered by the tip of the island. Bullets no longer came near them.

Setting a course toward the distant coast of one of the larger islands of the Luzon Union, Doc held the throttle wide. The boat, traveling at tremendous speed, jarred violently as it slammed across the tops of the choppy waves.

The corsair craft heaved around the end of the island. Once more bullets whistled about them. But they had gained considerably. Doc's men did not waste lead returning the fire.

Fifteen minutes of flight put them out of rifle shot.

Doc cut their speed.

"Hey!" Monk grunted. "We low on gas or somethin'? Those birds aren't giving up the chase!"

"Plenty of gas," Doc told him, and fell to watching their pursuers.

IT was a weird-looking flotilla which followed them. Behind the fast launches were the sampans. Then came the junks, such of them as were fitted with engines in addition to sail power. They strung out for miles. The most sluggish of the sailboats were hardly outside the corsair bay on Shark Head Island.

One launch began to draw ahead of the others.

Doc opened the throttle, spun their speed boat about, and raced for the boat which had left the others behind. But not a single bullet was exchanged. Their quarry dropped back with the other pirates.

Continuing their flight, Doc turned the controls over to Monk.

Working swiftly, Doc tugged bundle after bundle of soggy papers, loose-leaf notebooks and cards from his shirt front—the stuff Tom Too's brief case had held! He studied it with much interest.

"Anything worth while there?" Ham asked.

Elated little lights glowed in Doc's flaky golden eyes.

"Tom Too's organization was too large to keep track of without written records," he explained. "These are the records."

"A break, gettin' 'em, huh?" Monk grinned.

Not answering, Doc bent over the portable radio apparatus. He adjusted the dials. The tiny key was of the variety known as a sidewiper, requiring experience to manipulate. Doc fingered dots and dashes out of it with machinelike precision, then twirled the receiver dials, the headset pressed over his ears.

The noise of the launch motor prevented the others hearing what Doc was sending and receiving, although they were all expert operators. However, Doc began to consult notebooks and papers which had come from Tom Too's brief case. That explained what he was doing.

"He's gotten hold of a Mantilla station and is giving them the names of Tom Too's men in the city," Ham decided. "That should enable Juan Mindoro, with a handful of reliable police, to clean the pirates out of town."

After a time Doc laid Tom Too's records aside. But he continued to send and receive over the radio instruments, evidently carrying on a conversation with the distant station. Finally he ceased, and studied his men quietly.

"Want to take a big risk on the chance of destroying this pirate fleet?" he demanded.

"Sure!" Monk said promptly.

"Should the motor of this boat fail, it'd mean our finish!" Doc warned the men.

Monk made a gesture of patting the throbbing engine. "I'm willing to take that chance."

The others seemed of a like mind.

Doc resumed transmitting over the radio, and sent rapidly for some minutes. Then he deserted the apparatus and took over the launch controls.

Their boat now dawdled along just out of rifle range of the pursuers. Twice during the next two hours Doc swerved back as though to attack the leading launches of the yellow men. These retreated warily.

The hazy bulk of one of the larger islands of the Luzon Union heaved up ahead. Doc worked over the radio set. He seemed satisfied with the coded information which he had plucked out of the ether.

Swinging a wide circle, Doc and his men turned back for Shark Head Island. Like the tail on a slow comet, the pirate fleet followed.

Doc's boat was at least a dozen miles an hour faster than the swiftest of their pursuers. Several times bullets danced on the water near them, but the yellow men did not get close enough for accurate shooting.

The sun, which had blazed upon them with a heat that almost cooked, balanced like a red-hot stove lid above the evening horizon.

The corsair bay of Shark Head Island opened before the launch. The entire fleet manned by the slant-eyed men had been left behind.

Renny, standing erect to get the first glimpse into the bay, groaned: "Aw—blazes!"

On the shore of the little harbor stood a number of yellow cutthroats. These were ill or wounded pirates who had been left behind.

"They won't give us much trouble!" Doc decided.

Nor did they. Doc beached the launch some hundreds of yards from the Orientals. He sent a few long-range shots at the fellows to stop their charge, then plunged, along with his men, into the jungle.

With all sails set and engines laboring, the corsair vessels began reëntering the bay. Howling, brandishing weapons, yellow men dived into the jungle. They were highly elated. They couldn't understand why the big bronze man and his five aids had deliberately put themselves in a trap, but they did not give that much thought.

There was one exception—the buccaneers aboard the

largest of the junks, the vessel which was fitted lavishly with tapestries, paintings, rich rugs, and inlaid furniture. In the hold of this craft was a powerful engine.

It bore Tom Too himself. The master pirate did not land. Instead, after directing his men to pursue Doc, he ordered his junk to stand out to sea.

The Oriental craft was plowing through the mouth of the bay when a pair of speedy planes dropped out of the evening sky. Without the slightest hesitation, the aircraft loosened machine guns upon Tom Too's vessel.

Matting sails of the junk acquired great ragged rips. Splinters flew from the decks and hulls. Several of the crew dropped. Others replied to the machine-gun fire of the planes. A bomb, dropped by one of the aircraft, narrowly missed the junk, but made it roll sickeningly. The junk put back into the bay.

Out of the twilight haze that mantled the sea plunged several slender, gray, grim vessels. These were destroyers, little larger than submarine chasers, of the type that served the Luzon Union as a navy. Other planes appeared—giant tri-motored bombers and fast, single-engined pursuit ships.

The truth dawned on the yellow pirates. Instead of the bronze man being trapped, they were themselves cornered.

Doc had summoned aid by radio!

Chapter 22

RED BLADE

FROM the concealment of the jungle, Doc and his men watched developments.

"Juan Mindoro is aboard one of the planes," Doc declared. "At least, he should be, according to the information he gave me by radio."

"Can he depend on the men manning the planes and destroyers?" Ham questioned uneasily. "Tom Too may have some of them on his pay roll."

"He did have," Doc admitted. "But the records I got out of that brief case gave their names, and I passed the dope on to Mindoro. Tom Too's hirelings are under arrest."

Monk kneaded his enormous, furry hands. "How about us getting in this scrape?"

"We'll tackle that big junk," Doc agreed. "Tom Too is probably aboard."

The junk in question had hove to close to the beach. Yellow men were dropping a light boat overside, evidently to be used in ferrying Tom Too ashore. A bomb exploded in the bay, and the wall of water it flung out smashed the small boat against the junk hull.

Doc and his men ran for a sampan beached near by. They were fired upon, and returned the lead. A plane dived upon them, unable to distinguish them from foes in the increasing darkness. Doc led the others back into the jungle to evade the searching machine-gun metal. There they encountered a gang of a dozen desperate pirates. They fought, skulking in the jungle, each party shooting at the gun flashes of the other.

Plane motors bawled overhead. The planes flew so low that prop streams thrashed palm fronds. Detonating bombs made such concussions that the very island jumped and shuddered. Men yelled, cursed in an assorted score of dialects. Machine guns gobbled continuously.

"Kinda like old times!" Renny rumbled in the gloom.

Doc and his fellows rushed the yellow gang with whom they skirmished. Doc used only his hands in the scrap that followed. He moved like a bronze phantom. Man after man fell before his fists, or was rendered helpless with wrenched and broken limps. The pirate group broke and fled.

"To the sampan!" Doc's powerful voice commanded. "We'll make another try at reaching that big junk!"

They ran out on the beach, found the sampan, and shoved off.

Overhead, a plane dropped a parachute flare, then another. The calcium glare whitened the entire island.

The illumination showed Tom Too's junk trying to work out of the bay. Destroyers, however, blocked its escape. The hulking vessel turned back.

The flares sank fizzing into the sea and were extinguished. Bending to the sampan paddles, Doc's party headed for the junk.

"They won't expect to be boarded from a small boat," Renny boomed softly.

Doc guided the sampan expertly. They came alongside the junk in the gloom. A pirate saw them, hailed. Doc answered in a disguised tone, speaking the same dialect, telling the corsairs to hold their fire.

The sampan gunwale rasped along the junk hull. All six leaping at once, Doc's gang gained the deck of the larger vessel.

ANOTHER bomb, exploding harmlessly on the distant

beach, threw a flash like pale lightning. It disclosed Doc's identity.

A yellow man howled and leaped, swinging a short sword. Doc twisted from under the descending blade. His darting fist seemed a part of the same movement. The Oriental collapsed, his jaw hanging awry.

Fighting spread swiftly from end to end of the junk as Doc's men scattered. In the darkness, they could fight best when separated.

Doc himself made for the high, after part of the vessel, seeking Tom Too.

Below decks, the Orientals manning the engines became excited and threw the craft into full speed ahead. It plowed about aimlessly, no hand at the tiller.

Doc found a long bamboo pole, evidently a makeshift bat hook. He converted it to a weapon of offense, jabbing and swinging it in club fashion. A corsair bounced off the pole end as if he were a billiard ball, and tangled with one of his fellows.

The little machine guns had been latched back into rapid-fire. Once more they tore off series of reports so rapid they resembled the sound of coarse cloth tearing.

"One!" Doc barked.

"Two!" echoed Renny's strong voice. "Three!" said Long Tom. The others called off in rapid succession—four, five, six!

This was a procedure they followed often when fighting in the darkness. It not only showed the entire gang was still up and going, but also advised each man where the others were located.

Doc descended a carved companionway. He wanted to get the engines stopped before the junk crashed into some other craft.

He found the engine room without difficulty. Only two Orientals were there, huddling nervously under the pale glow of an electric lantern. They offered no fight at all, but threw down their weapons at Doc's sharp command. Doc shut off the motors.

"Where is Tom Too?" Doc asked.

The yellow men squirmed. They were scared. They had seen this giant bronze man slain by the sword and his body burned. Was he a devil, that he could come to life again?

One pointed toward the stern. "Maybe Tom Too, he go that dilection," he singsonged.

Doc made for the spot—the richly fitted quarters which were no doubt Tom Too's private rooms. Two Orientals barred his way. He was almost touching them before they were aware of his presence, so dark was the junk interior.

Doc shoved them both violently, and while they stumbled about and slashed viciously at black, empty air, he eased past them. There was movement ahead, and the glow of a flashlight.

A faint rasping sounded—a windowlike porthole of the junk being opened! It must be Tom Too, Doc knew. And the man was in the act of escaping from the junk into the waters of the bay.

Doc flung for the port—and had one of his narrowest escapes from death. Tom Too was easing through the porthole feet first. He turned his flashlight on Doc and threw a knife.

Doc saw the blade only when it glinted in the flash beam. He dodged, got partially clear. The blade lodged like a big steel thorn in his side, outside the ribs.

Tom Too dropped through the port. His madly splashing strokes headed for shore. Suddenly the splashing increased. A terrified scream pealed out.

Doc leaned from the porthole.

Overhead, a plane dropped another aërial flare. The blinding illumination it spread could not have been more timely, for the swimming figure of Tom Too was plainly disclosed.

A small shark had seized the pirate leader. Tom Too had no knife with which to defend himself this time—he had expended that on Doc. The corsair chief screeched and beat at the grisly monster which had fastened upon his leg.

The shark was but little longer than Tom Too. For a moment it seemed the pirate king would escape. Then a larger sea killer closed upon the human morsel.

Tom Too's distorted face showed plainly before he was submerged to his death.

The features were those of slender, dapper First Mate Jong of the ill-fated liner, *Malay Queen*.

It was dawn, and the sun blazed a flame of victory in the east. The fighting was over. A cowed, frightened cluster, the surviving pirates had been herded upon the beach and were under heavy guard, awaiting consignment to a penal colony.

The planes had managed to land on a level portion of the beach. Juan Mindoro had boarded the big junk. He was striving to express his gratitude to Doc Savage and the other five adventurers who had done so much for his native land.

"I have just received a radio message from Mantilla," he said, addressing Doc. "Thanks to the information in Tom

Too's records, which you gave us, the pirates in Mantilla have been captured, almost to a man. They even got Captain Hickman, of the *Malay Queen*. There is only one thing bothering me—are you certain Jong was Tom Too?"

"Positive," Doc told him. "The records disclosed that. Jong, or Tom Too, undoubtedly bribed Captain Hickman to sign him on the *Malay Queen* as first mate."

Mindoro ran a finger inside his collar and squirmed. "Words seem very flat when I try to express my thanks to you. I shall ask the Luzon Union government to appropriate a reward for——"

"Nix," Doc said.

Mindoro smiled, went on: "—a reward which I think you will accept."

Mindoro was right, for the reward was one Doc found entirely satisfactory. It consisted of a simple bronze plate bearing the plain words: "The Savage Memorial Hospital."

The plate was embedded in the cornerstone of a structure that cost millions. Other millions were placed in trust to insure operation of the hospital for years. The institution was to operate always under one inflexible rule—payment from no one but those who could afford it.

The laying of the cornerstone was accomplished with ceremony before Doc and his men left the Luzon Union.

Monk, uncouth in high hat and swallowtail coat, perspired under the derisive gaze of the dapper Ham throughout the ceremony. He was glad when it was over and they got out of the admiring crowd.

"Fooey!" snorted Monk, and made a present of his high silk hat to a brown-skinned, half-naked street urchin. "It'll take a good fight to get me feelin' like a human being again!"

Monk was going to get his fight, even if he didn't know it.

To the world at large, Doc Savage is a strange, mysterious figure of glistening bronze skin and golden eyes. To his fans he is the greatest adventure hero of all time, whose fantastic exploits are unequaled for hair-raising thrills, breathtaking escapes, blood-curdling excitement!

☐ THE EVIL GNOME	2134	$1.25
☐ THE MOUNTAIN MONSTER	2239	$1.25
☐ THE MAN OF BRONZE	6352	$1.25
☐ THE STONE MAN	6419	$1.25
☐ THE BOSS OF TERROR	6424	$1.25
☐ THE THOUSAND HEADED MAN	6471	$1.25
☐ THE RED TERRORS	6486	$1.25
☐ DOC SAVAGE: HIS APOCALYPTIC LIFE	8834	$1.25
☐ THE KING MAKER	10042	$1.25
☐ THE PHANTOM CITY	10119	$1.25
☐ THE MYSTIC MULLAH	10120	$1.25
☐ FEAR CAY	10121	$1.25
☐ LAND OF ALWAYS NIGHT	10122	$1.25
☐ FANTASTIC ISLAND	10125	$1.25
☐ QUEST OF QUI	10126	$1.25

Buy them at your local bookstore or use this handy coupon for ordering:

Bantam Book Catalog

Here's your up-to-the-minute listing of every book currently available from Bantam.

This easy-to-use catalog is divided into categories and contains over 1400 titles by your favorite authors.

So don't delay—take advantage of this special opportunity to increase your reading pleasure.

Just send us your name and address and 25¢ (to help defray postage and handling costs).